KATZ' CAT

BOOK 1 IN THE TWINKLE TEXAS COZY MYSTERY SERIES

DAWN GREENFIELD IRELAND

ARTISTIC
ORIGINS

❁ Formatted with Vellum

ACKNOWLEDGMENTS

February 2023 Review of Katz' Cat by Canadian author, Anne Shillolo.

I liked this book so much that I did not want it to end! Katz's Cat has it all. Sweet humor, lovable characters, talented pets, and a cast of memorable characters.

Is there really a place called Twinkle, Texas? I want to go there!

Main character Jimmy Katz is an honest, open-hearted reporter who decides to leave The Big City for a quieter life in Twinkle. It's not long before he finds out that even a small town can be hiding big secrets. And Jimmy finds himself at the center of a deadly conflict.

The mystery plot is complex, making the book a real page-turner, as we follow Jimmy, along with his new friends, loquacious parrot, and clever kitten, towards a surprise ending.

I hope this is a series and can't wait for Book 2. If you like books by Jana DeLeon or Lilian Jackson Braun, Katz's Cat will make your day!

A great cover says it all. Son #1, Brandon White of VictoryLaurel.com created the new series covers 5.2026.

Proofreaders find things by latching their laser eyes onto the page. I am so grateful for Jeff Gonyea and Richard (Grasshopper) Stone. They have whacked me with the wooden ruler dozens of times.

I love my little scene break icon designed by Fb Nyan. Let me know what you think.

Many thanks to @agus_kupit on Fiverr.com for creating the fabulous map of Twinkle, Texas.

Actions Appreciated

Please leave a review on the retailer website where you purchased the book, or on my website! Reviews help authors get recognized, get the word out, and sell more books. I will love you forever if you leave a review!

HINT: Don't regurgitate the synopsis for your review. Just tell people what you liked, didn't like. That's what people want... your opinion.

If you would like to join my **postcard brigade**, I'll mail you 4 postcards. One for you and three to hand out. Email me your address and I'll mail them to you. USA only. All others, I can email you the postcard for sharing with your world.

Every word I have written and published is from my noggin (brain, in case you don't know what noggin means). My fiction is all make-believe, from the deep dive into my wild imagination. All my nonfiction books have been researched until my brain has scrambled.

Nonfiction	
The Puppy Baby Book	Mastering Your Money (2022)
Puppy Adoption and Beyond	Writers Preparation Handbook
Mastering Your Money (2008)	What's Breaking Your Budget
Online Classes	
Writers Preparation Handbook	How to Format Word Docs Like A Pro
Cozy Mysteries	**Sci-Fi-Fantasy**
The Alcott Family Adventures	**The Thol Series**
Hot Chocolate	Prophecy of Thol
Bitter Chocolate	Gifts From Thol
Spicy Chocolate	Love of Thol
Nutty Chocolate	King of Thol
Katz' Cat Series	Earth Calling Thol
Katz' Cat	**Sci-Fi Romance Adventure**
Bill Hill's Pills	Forced Dreams
The Detectives	**Dystopian**
Coming in 2025: The Pact	The Last Dog
	Texmexzona
Books by my Alter Ego ~ DG Ireland	
Bonded Shapeshifter Billionaire Series	
Bonded	
Tothars	
Tilted	
Unforeseen	
Connected	
Need A Notebook?	
See my 54 themed notebooks on my website	
www.degreenfield.com/notebooks	
Screenplays formatted as books	
Plan B (Dark Comedy)	Where's Ralphie? (Family Comedy)
The God Child (Action Adventure)	Standing Dead (Drama/Tragedy)
The Far Corner (Sci-Fi/Psychological/Creatures)	
Screenplays as TV Episodes	
Hot Chocolate ~ Episode 1	Prophecy of Thol ~ Episode 1
Bonded ~ Episode 1	
See my screenplays on my website: degreenfield.com	
Filmfreeway, CoverFly, ISA Network	

GETTING AROUND TWINKLE

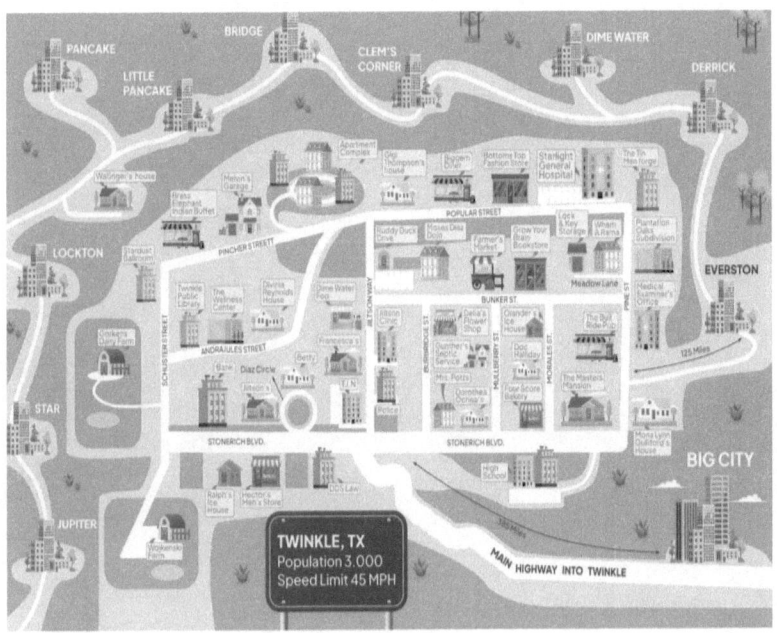

THE HUMAN CHARACTERS...

Jimmy Katz, the main character in the Katz' Cat / Twinkle, TX cozy mystery book series

Mrs. Potts, the boardinghouse landlady in the Katz' Cat / Twinkle, TX cozy mystery book series

Chief Price in the Katz' Cat / Twinkle, TX cozy mystery book series

Brian, Jimmy's best friend from the Big City who moves to Twinkle in the Katz' Cat / Twinkle, TX cozy mystery

CHAPTER ONE

J immy Katz drove his late-model Honda CR-V with a periwinkle blue paint job along twisted roads to Twinkle, Texas, 385 miles from the closest shopping mall. All four windows were down at least six inches, blowing his sandy hair about. The town lived in Starlight County, which was the second county established in the old Republic of Texas.

His journey started from Houston on I-10 heading west. After a couple of hundred miles, he decided to add scenery and traveled county roads heading northwest, west and southwest. It was a dizzying drive along two-lane roads that reminded him of a drunken snake he once found in his backyard as a child.

Guppy, Jimmy's green Amazon parrot with a blue splotch over his beak between his eyes and bright yellow feathers at the base of his neck, was the designated backseat driver. The bird came to have an immense and colorful vocabulary from his previous owner. Boxes, bags, and suitcases hemmed in Guppy's travel cage. He squawked in indignation when a vehicle zoomed past the CR-V speeding. "Slow down, you numbskull!"

Jimmy checked the rearview mirror, then both side mirrors. He flipped his signal light to pass a farmer on a tractor, then sped up and got around him before an 18-wheeler roared past in the opposite direction on the four-lane road. The farmer tooted his horn and waved. Jimmy waved back, one of the good-natured experiences of the Texas countryside.

"You know, Guppy, if we were still in The Big City, that farmer would have waved his middle finger at us," Jimmy said, his baby blue eyes lit with humor.

"To hell with 'em! To hell with 'em!" Guppy squawked.
"You got that right, buddy. I'm so done with The Big City,"

Jimmy said. He thought back on this life-changing move
and what brought it about. He had covered a story for The Big
City paper which took him to I-45 N. He pulled o# the high-
way, stopped at a gas station and filled up his car.

Just as he tightened the gas cap, three thugs approached
him, one waving a gun in his face. They took his money and his
keys. He begged them to let him have his briefcase. As they got
in Jimmy's car and drove o#, a window buzzed down and the
briefcase !ew out and bounced along the ground before coming
to a stop just a short distance from where Jimmy was kneeling.

He was so shook up, he could barely pull his cellphone out
of his pocket. The manager of the gas station ran out of the
convenience store, followed by several customers.

"Are you okay, man?" the manager asked. "I called the
cops."

"Thanks. I can't believe they robbed me at gunpoint,"
Jimmy said as he stood.

A customer brought him his briefcase. "You're lucky they
were in a charitable mood. Typically, they don't let you have
anything."

Three weeks later, the cops called. They found his vehicle,
barely recognizable after being torched. Then he discovered the insurance company paid the actual cash value for his
CR-V, and didn't pay o! the note. His head spun the problem.
He didn't know how he would get into another vehicle while
still having to pay the current balance on his fried car.

Jimmy was in the process of spiraling downward with the
enormous problem those thugs presented. He didn't make a lot
of money. He didn't have any backup plan. He didn't have any
family to fall back on. Brian McKinley, his one true friend from
way back in kindergarten, was o! on a sabbatical somewhere

trying to find himself after a bad breakup. Jimmy had been okay with his life until a month ago. As long as he had a roof over his head, and he and Guppy had food, he was satis#ed.

The only other time in his life when things hit rock bottom was when he was between jobs for a little longer than he expected. He had to rent a storage unit for his meager possessions after he was evicted, and he and Guppy were forced to live in the storage unit, hiding from the security and management staff.

He shook o! that bad memory as he drove the rental car to the newspaper, turned in his resignation, cleared out his desk and went home to his apartment. He took a week to decompress from reliving the experience of identifying his vehicle.

"Guppy, we're getting out of the city and moving to the country. I hope I can find a good place for us to live where I'll build you a fenced-in area and you can be outside whenever you want, okay?"

"Freedom!" Guppy squawked from his perch on a suspended fake log in a corner of the tiny living room. Jimmy had papered the floor with old newspapers in a wide circumference around the bird. Parrot hygiene was very important to Jimmy.

FINALLY, his luck turned. Someone was selling their mother's Honda CR-V. It had low mileage, was in pristine condition and they only wanted fifteen hundred dollars. He could make it work.

The Twinkle Independent News (TIN) was a biweekly paper that published on Wednesdays and Saturdays. They were looking for an experienced journalist to fill a recently retired news veteran's slot. When Jimmy came across the Help Wanted ad online, he immediately sent them his resume. He received an email less than 24-hours later with a Zoom link for an interview.

His interview with Bill Trance, a fifty-something managing editor with an upbeat personality, went smoothly. The pay wasn't all that great, but the cost of living would be much lower than The Big City, so it would all work out. He accepted the job. Trance suggested a couple of places Jimmy could check out for temporary lodging until he got the lay of the land.

So, here he was, on the road to Twinkle, Texas, on the outskirts of civilization, leaving all the downsides of high population, bumper-to-bumper traffic, deafening noise, and heavy pollution behind him when his phone rang.

"Hello? Who is this?" he asked when Unknown showed on Caller ID.

"Jimzer! It's me," Brian said through a crackly connection.

"Where are you?"

"Bri? Where the heck have you been? My life's turned upside down. Guppy and I are on the way to Twinkle," Jimmy shouted into the phone.

"What happened? I went by your place and it's vacant, man! Twinkle? Is that in Texas?"

Jimmy explained the situation and promised to call him when they got situated. "Text me your new number. It didn't come through."

"GUPPY, THEY HAVE SOME STRANGE NAMES FOR TOWNS out in the country," Jimmy said. "We'll have to check out Jupiter, Star, Clem's Corner and Pancake. Who would have thought we'd be moving to a town named Twinkle in Starlight County?"

"Time to eat," Guppy squawked.

"No, it isn't," Jimmy said. "Hey, look—there's an oil derrick way over there!"

He drove for another thirty miles, then passed the sign for Twinkle that showed Population, 3,000. He slowed his speed to the required 45-mph and kept his eyes peeled for the directions to Mrs. Potts' house on Burbridge Street. GPS told him to take the next right. Then his destination would be on the right at 400 feet.

Jimmy found the large two-story white rooming house, pulled his vehicle up at the curb, and parked. "You wait here, Guppy. I'll go meet with Mrs. Potts and see where we're going to stay."

"Time to eat!" Guppy squawked.

"We'll eat as soon as we're settled," Jimmy said as he got out of the car and walked up the walkway lined with fragrant herbs. He had never seen mint, fennel, parsley, rosemary, thyme, or oregano grown in such abundance. He climbed the two steps and rang the doorbell.

The door opened, and a stout, fiftyish woman with shocking white, spiked hair and streaks of purple greeted him.

"Mr. Katz?" she asked in a moderately loud voice. "That's me. Please call me Jimmy," he said.

She opened the door wider and invited him inside. She glanced at his car. "Will your bird be okay in the car?"

"Oh, sure. The windows are halfway down. He'll be okay for a little while," Jimmy said.

"Do you think you'd prefer the upstairs apartment or the ground floor?" Mrs. Potts asked.

"Can I see them first? I don't have much with me, but I want to see what Guppy's views would be," he said.

JIMMY SETTLED Guppy's travel cage in a corner of the living room between two windows. One was a view of the backyard where he noticed a vegetable garden. The other was the side of the property with a mature oak tree with squirrel activity.

He hauled his boxes, bags, suitcases, and his laptop case out of the vehicle and up the stairs, and got to work unpacking. The apartment was comfortably furnished with an overstuffed sofa, a recliner, two end tables, a coffee table, a 36-inch TV on a stand, and an empty bookcase. A desk was against the wall. He set his briefcase on the desk, moved a box of "les and office supplies beside it then carried his book boxes to the bookcase.

The bedroom featured a queen bed with a high headboard, two nightstands, a dresser, and a chest of drawers. It was more than he would ever need, but he liked the setup. The bathroom contained a clawfoot tub plus a shower stall, two sinks, a bunch of drawers and cabinets under the long counter, and his and hers closets. He discovered the toilet behind another door.

He had really lucked out with the accommodations. There was a small kitchen with all the amenities: a gas stove, a refrigerator, a dishwasher, a microwave, a small pantry with a can of corn, a kitchen table, and four chairs. He opened cabinets and found

dishes, cups, glasses, pots and pans, and silverware. Another door hid a vacuum, broom, dust mop and dustpan, a bucket and mop.

He was thankful that all the floors were a rich, honey-colored hardwood—the real stuff, not engineered. Jimmy loathed carpeting. It was a cesspool for nasty bacteria that caused the majority of all allergies. The apartment had several nice throw and area rugs that would be easy to care for.

"Waiter! Waiter! Where's my food?" Guppy squawked. "Just hold on," Jimmy said. "I'm going to set up your area, and then I'll get your food and water. I've got to go grocery shopping and stock up with people and bird food."

Jimmy made another couple of trips out to the vehicle. He assembled the three pieces of Guppy's tree, which brought the height to five feet, then the other two pieces that were the cross branches. Once everything was together, he placed it between the two corner windows. Then he attached Guppy's food dish holder and stainless water bowl holder. He dug old newspapers out of the box and papered the floor.

"Okay, big guy. Here's your new place. Do you like it?" He opened the travel cage, and the bird climbed onto his arm. He walked over to the tree, and Guppy climbed onto his perch and checked out the windows.

Jimmy tackled putting together Guppy's sleeping and activity cage. It was a huge wire cage with a hanging rope, wood perches, and food and water cups. It took a while to put it together. He also attached the bird's favorite toys where he liked them. Almost an hour later, the cage was completely assembled.

Jimmy rolled the cage to the end of one of the fake tree branches. When his bird wanted to play or go to bed, he could walk across the branch into his cage.

Guppy squawked indignantly. "Where's the food?"

Jimmy tore into a box and pulled out a package of Guppy's favorite seed mix. "You'll have your veggies and fruit when I get back from the store." He took the water bowl to the kitchen sink and filled it, then settled it into the metal attachment on the fake tree. "Be back later."

He locked the apartment door, headed down the stairs and out the door. Jimmy had never lived anywhere that had a garden or herbs growing, and he appreciated this new country life where the air was so aromatic from herbs that he automatically inhaled.

The journalist turned the car around and headed back to the main street, Stonerich Boulevard. He decided to stop at the paper before grabbing a bite to eat, to see where he'd be work-ing, and to meet his new boss. GPS told him to make a left on Jiltson Way, and his destination would be on the right.

Jimmy parked the car in front of the Twinkle Independent News building. It was an old tan brick building with windows along the front and huge wooden double doors. He went inside and was greeted by a middle-aged receptionist wearing a Bose headset. One hand typed, another copied as she rolled her chair as if on a speedway behind a six-foot command center with three 32-inch monitors, a gigantic flashing keyboard and a fax/copier. One monitor displayed her typing. The other two showed security pictures of Jiltson Way, the front door, back door, and the parking lot.

Ten feet behind her was the newsroom floor.

The nameplate on the counter read Millicent Montoya. "Hi, may I help you?" she asked.

"I'm Jimmy Katz..."

"Oh! You're the new reporter! Let me call Bill. Welcome to the TIN!" she blurted as she worked the switchboard. "Bill, Mr. Katz is here." She looked up at Jimmy. "He's on his way."

Jimmy perused the framed headlines on the wall: Twinkle Derricks beat Clem's Corner Buckshot's 10-2. Mitch Ogilvie's 100th Birthday. Bertha Potts Wins FFAs Herb Competition Hands Down. He stared at the headlines as if they were in a foreign language he couldn't understand. No murders, rapes, robberies.

"I'll bet those are a little different from the headlines you're used to," Bill Trance said.

Jimmy jumped. He hadn't heard the managing editor approach. They shook hands.

"There's no crime headlines," Jimmy said, mildly shocked. "You'll get used to country living in no time," Bill said. "Let me show you where your desk is, then we can go to lunch."

They walked through the room that was the heart of the paper. Several unoccupied desks showed active use with stacks of notes, newspaper clippings, file folders, and whatnot. There were four offices along a wall. A large map of the area and a map of the United States covered a wall. A whiteboard was on another wall. He noticed a jumble of large conference tables throughout the room.

Bill walked up to a desk that held an office phone, wire baskets, a pencil cup, and a lined tablet in the middle of the clean surface. "Here's your new desk, Jimmy. If you stop back by before six, you can meet some of your coworkers." He steered Jimmy to the offices along the wall. "This is my office. Door's always open. Want to grab a bite to eat?"

"That would be great. Where's a grocery store? I need to stock up. My bird expects me to bring home his fruit and veggies."

"What kind of bird do you have?" Bill asked.

"Amazon parrot named Guppy, and he's a talker," Jimmy said.

"Did you settle into Mrs. Potts' place?" Bill asked.

"Yes. Thanks so much for the recommendation. It's clean, quiet and just the right size. Guppy has a good view from two windows," Jimmy said.

As they left Bill's office, he pointed to a door. "That's the door to the parking lot," Bill said. "Milly, we're going to Francesca's."

"Okay, boss," Milly said with a wave.

They walked next door to a cafe with a huge plate-glass window. Bill didn't wait to be seated. He walked over to a booth and slid onto the seat, with Jimmy sitting across from him. He reached over to the wall at the end of the booth where plastic-coated menus were behind the condiments.

Bill handed a menu to Jimmy. As they were perusing their choices, a buxom woman padded over to the table.

"Hey, Bill. Do you want to know the special for today?" she asked.

"Hi Francesca. This is my new reporter, Jimmy Katz. He's not from around here, so give him a break," Bill said, with a wink. "What's the special?"

Francesca grinned. "Hi, Jimmy. Today's special is a double patty cheese burger with bacon and my special sauce, a side of either fries or onion rings, and a drink. Should I give you a minute to look over the menu?"

"The special sounds good to me. I'll have onion rings," Jimmy said.

"You know what I want," Bill said.

"Two specials coming up," Francesca said. Jimmy frowned across the table at Bill.

"The special is the same every day. In other words, there isn't a special," Bill said.

"Oh, okay," Jimmy said.

"When you come in tomorrow, ask Milly for your press card and a window sticker for your car. That way you won't have to worry about getting yelled at by the police or any other officials until they get to know you. Then, all bets are o"," Bill said. "Make sure you keep your receipts for any expenses while you cover your assignment. You turn those in to Milly with an expense report. Oh, and ask her for a map of Starlight County. Sometimes GPS doesn't work out in the boondocks."

"How many towns do we cover?" Jimmy asked.

"Aside from Twinkle, there are eight towns: Jupiter, Star, Clem's Corner, Lockton, Pancake, Bridge, Derrick, and Dime Water. You'll get to know your way around in no time," Bill said.

Francesca carried two heaping plates to the table. "Two specials. Let me know if you need anything else."

Jimmy looked at his plate. He had never seen such a huge burger. "Thanks. This looks great!"

"Homemade buns to fit the burgers," Francesca said proudly.

Jimmy grabbed his knife and cut the burger in half. Even that was a handful. He and Bill chomped and chewed. The onion rings were good. Nice and crisp.

"This is great! I don't think I can finish this huge burger," Jimmy said.

"Supper. A two-fer-one deal," Bill said. "Now, for coffee and breakfast, you might want to try the Four Score bakery. They have great coffee choices and good breakfasts. Francesca's isn't open for breakfast."

"Where's the bakery?" Jimmy asked. "Morales Street. You can't miss it," Bill said.

They finished lunch. Bill paid for both of them. When they were outside, he pointed out the driveway to the rear parking lot.

"Where's a grocery store?" Jimmy asked.

"Dime Water Food store is around the block. The sign is missing the D on Food so it reads Foo," Bill said.

They shook hands on the sidewalk, and Jimmy drove around the block to the grocery store.

JIMMY MADE two trips from the car to the apartment with groceries. He hunted for a colander to wash the produce and finally found one stuck in a big pot in a lower cabinet. He hunted down a chopping mat for the veggies and fruit. He found a set of plastic mats in different colors: green for produce, yellow for poultry, blue for seafood, and red for meat. Then he got busy making Guppy's bin of vegetables. He prepared a separate bin with fruit the bird loved.

"Waiter, waiter, where's my food?" the bird squawked.

"Hold your horses. You can see me in the kitchen fixing it for you," Jimmy said.

"Fix it! Fix it!" the bird bellowed. He had a good pair of lungs.

Jimmy filled the plate with chopped asparagus, mushrooms, carrots, broccoli, spinach, and orange bell peppers. He tossed in red seedless grapes, orange slices, and chunks of banana.

"Here you go. Enjoy!" he said as he placed the plate inside the special metal holder on Guppy's tree. "I'm going to do some more unpacking."

Jimmy eyed the desk, then the bookcase across the room. He moved the bookcase close to the desk and unpacked his books, which included *Words on Words*, *The Newspapers Handbook*, *Doing Ethics in Journalism*, *Essential Researcher*, *Associated Press Stylebook and Libel Manual*, *The New York Times Manual of Style and Usage*, and the *Chicago Manual of Style*.

He set up the desk and unpacked his office supplies. He found his laptop charger, hunted for a receptacle, and plugged the charger into the computer. Once that was all to his liking,

he grabbed a beer out of the fridge, flopped onto the sofa and grabbed the remote.

"Let's see what's on TV," he said. He discovered Net!ix was available, so he flipped through the choices and settled on a mystery. Weary from the long trip, he dozed o" for a while. When he woke, he shut the TV o", checked on Guppy, who was already in his sleep cage, and he went to bed.

CHAPTER TWO

The alarm on Jimmy's cellphone blared. In the other room, Guppy moved from his sleeping cage to his fake tree and looked out the windows. He drank water and perused his empty plate.

"Waiter, waiter, where's my food?" he blared.

Jimmy turned over, grabbed his phone, stopped the alarm and checked the time. He flung his feet over the edge of the bed and trudged over to Guppy. He swiped a hand over the bird's head, grabbed the empty plate and the water bowl.

"Be right back, buddy."

He washed the plate and bowl, prepared Guppy's breakfast of fruit and veggies, which included some sweet potato the parrot was especially fond of, and refilled the water bowl.

"Breakfast's ready!" Jimmy called out.

"About time!" Guppy squawked.

Jimmy retreated to the kitchen, started a pot of coffee, grabbed a frying pan and cooked four scrambled eggs. His cooking skills were mediocre, but at least he wouldn't starve.

"Time for a shower. You ready?" Jimmy asked Guppy.

"Bath time!" the parrot squawked out.

He brought Guppy to the bathroom. "Let me get the water going." Once the water was the right temperature, Jimmy placed Guppy's bath stand in the shower stall and held his arm out for the bird to hop onto the stainless-steel stand.

The bird flapped his wings, snapped at the water with his beak, and had a good time.

Jimmy showered and washed his hair, then shut the water o#.

"Awk! Water! Water!" Guppy squawked.

"You've had enough water," Jimmy said. He grabbed a towel and wiped his face, hair, then wrapped the towel around his waist. He grabbed a smaller towel and rubbed it lightly over the parrot. "Stay there while I shave."

Jimmy finished with his bathroom routine. He dressed in a suit and tie and got ready for his first day at his new job. He walked Guppy back to his fake tree in the living room. Before leaving, Jimmy unplugged the coffee maker and checked the thermostat to make sure Guppy would be comfortable.

"See you later, Guppy. I'm heading out to start my new job.

Make sure you supervise the squirrels and birds." "Awk," the bird squawked. "On the job!"

JIMMY DROVE THE HONDA INTO THE PARKING LOT FOR the TIN and entered the back door. He stopped at Milly's desk.

"Hi Milly. Bill said you'd have my press card," he said.

"Welcome aboard, Jimmy." Milly handed him a Manila folder. "Make sure you put the windshield stickers on the inside. It's one of those clear things that peels o# for easy placement. I give everyone two so they can stick one on the front and rear windows. Better to have them visible coming and going.

The phone list is in there. Better plug the numbers into your phone so you know who's calling."

She dragged a laptop case across the counter and hefted it up to the reporter. "Here's your MacBook Pro. There's a bunch of paperwork I need you to fill out and sign in your packet."

Her phone rang. She gave him the thumbs-up as she answered with, "Thanks for calling the Twinkle Independent News. How can I direct your call?"

Jimmy grabbed the laptop case and the envelope and waved at Milly, then walked into the inner workings of the paper. He found his desk and got busy setting up. He was the only one in the room, which he thought was strange.

Moments later, a guy in a sports jacket, jeans and cowboy boots approached his desk. "Hey, we've just started our catchup meeting and Bill said you probably didn't know."

Jimmy stuck out his hand. "Oh! Jimmy Katz." They shook hands.

"Danny Stonerich."

They walked to the conference room. Danny slipped into his seat and took a sip of his coffee. Jimmy felt his collar tightening as all eyes were upon him.

Bill stood, walked up to Jimmy, and patted his back. "Everyone welcome Jimmy Katz. He's Herb's replacement and comes to us from The Big City, so he has plenty of experience. He's not used to country life, so be gentle."

There were some tittering and outright guffaws at Jimmy's expense.

Bill turned to the older man, who had been writing on the whiteboard. "This is Sylvan Stonerich, the editor and publisher of the TIN."

Sylvan crossed the room and shook Jimmy's hand. "Welcome, Jimmy. I hope you have a long and fulfilling career with us. You finding your way around town okay?"

"I haven't really had time to explore yet, but I know where to get breakfast, lunch and groceries, thanks to Bill," he said.

Bill went around the room introducing people: Gert Pruptek, a thin 40-something with penciled eyebrows above her shaved brow line. She looked as if she'd blow away with a high wind. Gert was in charge of sales, classifieds, and circulation.

Eddie Garcia was the production layout person and the go-to tech support guy who had one of those big black ear plugs in his right ear. He also kept the TIN website up to date.

Kingston (Deuce) Bainbridge, wearing a t-shirt with the number 14 in big blue letters, sported a tan from his many sports activities, and had a sparkling smile. He covered the sports beat.

The staff writers included Gigi Thompson, a natural blonde with shapely white-blonde eyebrows, big blue eyes, and a knockout figure. Her revealing blouse, form-fitted crop pants, and three-inch high heels spoke volumes as she gazed wide-eyed at being introduced to the new reporter.

Agatha (Ag) Diaz, a 50ish cowgirl type of woman, wore her long, undulating brunette hair down the middle of her back. She looked like a laid-back, carefree person in jeans, short deco-rated boots, a t-shirt and a jeans vest. Ag was a 15-year veteran staff writer with the TIN.

He had already met Danny Stonerich, a staff writer. Jimmy wondered if he was related to the big man.

After introductions, the meeting commenced with Sylvan at the whiteboard.

Mable Pinchmore was suing Dusty Burbridge. Danny was assigned to get to the bottom of the problem.

Gigi would cover the Bottoms Top story. Marivelle Twin-ster, the owner of the fashion store, had taken out a full-page ad for the store's new inventory which was sure to cause a stir.

It was the closest thing to Victoria's Secret the country town had.

Ag would head out to Pancake to discover if the Gorken's cow had really given birth to a two-headed calf, or if it was a hoax.

Deuce was covering the home baseball game between Twinkle and Clem's Corner.

Gert snippily suggested that Gigi might consider taking

photos *this time, that is, if her cellphone managed to not leap into another toilet.* It looked to Jimmy that an undercurrent existed between the two women, and to get between them would be dangerous as the high-velocity verbal shrapnel flung around. Bill managed to diffuse the situation by suggesting Gert accompany Gigi and take the photos herself. The older woman gloated with satisfaction.

The meeting broke up and Jimmy headed to his desk to empty the manila envelope, fill out the forms, load his cellphone with the TIN and other numbers. He also had to log into the laptop to see what software was loaded. He left the TIN at 11:10 and headed over to the library on Andrajules Street to talk to Divinia Reynolds about the summer programs.

DIVINIA REYNOLDS WAS A STATELY, FULL-figured woman in a flattering blue dress with white polka dots and shirring at the waist. The 50ish woman was all business. Her office was on the second floor at the top of the stairs, and the glass walls gave her a bird's-eye view of the two floors so she could easily keep track of patrons, employees, and volunteers.

"I've taken the liberty to pull some books for you," Divinia said as she handed him the first book. "This is a history of Twinkle and the leading families. Here's a book that covers the

entire Starlight County. When you're not from here, you won't know the histories or the people. And I don't know how much you know about oil and gas, but I'm going to assume you've noticed derricks as you drove into town. This book will give you a heads-up about the O&G industry here in Starlight County."

Jimmy was grateful for the thoughtfulness of the woman. He was in new territory and wasn't well equipped with the goings-on in country towns and the surrounding county. The closest he had come to the country was Pearland, Texas, which wasn't anything to sneeze at, with a population around a hundred-thousand.

They discussed the planned summer programs: the summer reading program (all age groups), creating with PVC pipe, cooking basics, intermediate cooking, creating a dream board, and careers in oil and gas.

He thanked her and headed back to the office, where he commenced to write up details about the programs so he wouldn't forget. He wondered if Bill wanted a block with the class titles, days and times with brief descriptions of each, or something more engaging.

Jimmy stopped by Bill's office where he found the managing editor chomping down on a sandwich and reading a rival newspaper with a red pen. He furiously circled something and glared at the page.

"Hi, boss. Thought I'd let you know that I met with Divinia and got the details about the summer program," Jimmy said.

"Look at these errors! If our newspaper had these kinds of mistakes, I'd #re someone!" Bill slurped his milkshake and calmed down. "How'd it go? Divinia's a gem."

"She was very helpful. Did you want the summer program courses in a big block, or do you want me to add write-ups and pictures I can find on the web?" he asked.

"How about the basics in the big block, and a sidebar with details and pictures? Eddie has unlimited space for the website, but we only have ten pages in print," Bill said.

"Okay, I'll get on it," Jimmy said.

"Make sure you lock up your laptop when you go home," Bill said.

"No problem. I have a MacBook Pro at home, and I can email my work back and forth," Jimmy said.

Bill nodded his approval, picked up the red pen and tackled the next page with glee.

JIMMY CLIMBED THE STAIRS TO HIS APARTMENT AND unlocked the door. "I'm home!"

The apartment was quiet. He crossed the floor to the desk and set the library books down. Guppy's tree and sleeping cage were empty. A tightening in his chest gripped him as he called out to the bird, frantic.

"Guppy?"

He raced about, checking the windows. They were secure. He entered his empty bedroom, then tore into the bathroom. The Amazon parrot was nowhere to be found. Jimmy raced down the stairs to Mrs. Potts' place. He heard the bird before seeing him.

Mrs. Potts was shelling peas at the kitchen table while Guppy sat perched on one of the chairs. She rolled a pea across the table, and his bird snatched it up in his beak.

"Guppy! I liked to have a heart attack when I couldn't find you!" Jimmy calmed himself with a couple of practiced breaths. He looked to his landlady for an explanation.

"I'm so sorry to have scared you. I take it you didn't see the note I left on the table?"

He shook his head.

"I was pulling weeds in the garden and kept hearing this tapping sound. Too loud for a woodpecker, and we don't get many around here. I looked all over the place, then I saw your bird in the window," she explained. "When I moved to the side of the house, he tapped on that window. I wanted to make sure nothing was the matter. We've had a good time—he's very entertaining!"

"That he is. I hope he didn't say anything inappropriate," Jimmy said. "His former owner had quite a racy vocabulary."

"I promise not to scare you again. How about I text you if he wants company?" Mrs. Potts asked.

"That would be great. Would I be able to build an enclosure in the backyard so he can be outside evenings and weekends when I don't have to work?" Jimmy asked.

"You know what? I've been wanting a gazebo for a while now. My nephews, George and Jerry, could tackle this project. They build things," Mrs. Potts said. "I'll tell them to get started on it."

"Let me know how much they'd charge. I'll be able to pay in installments, if that's okay with you," Jimmy said.

She waved a hand at him. "Psshh. Don't even think about it. I'll expense it as part of my boarding house, and I'll make sure it's tightly screened with a good strong pneumatic door closer."

"What do you think, Guppy?" Jimmy asked. "You're going to be able to go outside!"

"Freedom!" the bird squawked.

"I've been promising him this for a while now. Just couldn't make it happen in The Big City—he'd most likely end up stolen," Jimmy said.

"You don't have to worry about that here," Mrs. Potts said. "I'm not saying theft doesn't happen in Twinkle, but the

grapevine would know about it pretty quick, and it's not like you could hide a bird like this for long."

Jimmy held his arm out to Guppy. "Ready to go home and spend time together?"

"Yup! Go Home!" Guppy belched out.

"Oh, before I forget. If you ever have need of a veterinarian, Doc Halliday's office is over on Elizabeth Avenue," Mrs. Potts said.

"Good to know. I like to always keep a vet on hand in case of emergencies." He said goodbye, then coaxed Guppy to climb on his arm, and they went upstairs.

Jimmy walked over to Guppy's perch, and the parrot hopped onto his tree. He looked out the window at the old oak tree.

"Invaders!" he squawked.

"The squirrels are not invading us," Jimmy said. He went to the kitchen and spotted the note on the table. He didn't know how he missed it. *I'm babysitting your bird downstairs.*

He prepared Guppy's meal and replenished the water, then looked in the fridge for himself.

"I'm going out to explore the town and get something to eat," Jimmy said. "I won't be gone long."

"Long gone!"

Jimmy headed out the door and locked it behind him. First, he headed over to the grocery store where the gas station was located and filled the tank. Then he drove around and spotted a sign for The Bull Ride Pub. He wondered if they offered food. He pulled into the parking lot.

A colorful mechanical bull was bolted to the floor in the middle of the place. There was a wide berth between the bull and the tables, and the patrons chatted up a storm.

After his eyes adjusted to the interior, he approached the vacant stand where a sign instructed patrons to wait to be

seated. A young woman with a name tag that read Annie, rushed over to the stand and appraised the guest with eyes that screamed *I'm husband hunting!*

"Welcome to the Bull Ride. Is there just one in your party, or are you expecting someone to join you?" she asked.

"It's just me," he said. "Do you serve meals, or is this just a pub—I'm new here."

Annie captured him with a wide smile. "Oh, welcome to

Twinkle! When did you arrive? And to answer your question, yes, we have a full menu of choices, which are great—take my word for it! Let's get you seated."

Jimmy answered as she guided him to a table. "I just arrived yesterday, so I'm learning my way around."

Annie placed the menu on a table, and Jimmy pulled out a chair and sat. "Horace will be with you soon—he's the best waiter," she whispered.

"Thanks," Jimmy said, not sure why he deserved this special treatment. He studied the menu, then let his eyes explore the interior of the pub. On one wall was a mural of a Texas longhorn bull. If he had to venture a guess, he'd say those horns spanned at least seven or eight feet. He wondered how the animals balanced all that weight on their heads.

A waiter with smiling eyes approached his table. "Hey, I'm Horace. Annie said you're new to town. Are you new to Texas?"

"Hi, Horace. I grew up in The Big City. Wanted a slower, saner pace," Jimmy said.

"It's slower here, for sure," Horace said. "Not sure about the saner part. You'll have to weigh in after you've been here for a while. What could I get you?"

"I'll take the shepherd's pie. There was a pub where I used to eat all the time that had the best shepherd's pie, but they closed after many years at the same location," Jimmy said.

"Would you like a salad to go with that?" "No, thanks."

"Okay. It's a short wait, but someone will bring a bread-basket and butter. Would you want iced tea or something from the bar?"

"Tea is great," Jimmy said.

Horace rushed o" toward the kitchen, and a waiter appeared with the breadbasket and a plate of sliced butter. He returned a moment later with a glass of iced tea.

Jimmy chose a warm corn muffin and smeared it with butter. As he bit into the muffin, he let his eyes wander around the room again. He spotted a table with three women who smiled widely as his eyes caught each of theirs. He self-consciously wiped his mouth with the napkin, all the while wondering what they were smiling at. The reporter averted his eyes and focused on a cluster of framed pictures across the way.

Annie seated a couple of men at the table next to his. She stopped by his table. "Everything okay? Can I get you anything?"

Jimmy smiled up at her. "Thanks. Everything's under control. Good corn muffins."

She wandered back to her place by the front door. A few minutes later, Horace approached his table with a steaming crock filled with shepherd's pie. "Very hot," he said while placing the bowl on the table.

"That looks and smells wonderful," Jimmy said as he inspected the perfectly browned mashed potatoes covering the rich meat filling.

"What type of work do you do?" Horace inquired for the bene%t of the three women who had bribed him with ten bucks.

"Just started work at the newspaper," Jimmy said. "I'm Jimmy Katz."

Horace extended his hand and they shook. "Good to meet you, Jimmy. Hope you like our shepherd's pie." He stopped off at the table of the women, whispered the intel, then was waylaid by Annie who threatened him with bodily harm if he didn't share what he had learned from the newcomer.

All that was oblivious to Jimmy as he dug into the crock. He had to control his eyes from rolling up and back at his first taste. His tastebuds told him that the Bull Ride's offering far surpassed The Big City fare. A waiter refreshed his iced tea and disappeared again. After scraping the last morsel of tantalizing goodness from the crock, he sat back and sighed.

Jimmy sipped his tea. Horace approached again. "Ready for dessert? We have a molten chocolate brownie, homemade butter pecan ice cream, a couple of different cheesecakes, and apple pie."

"You are definitely trying to fatten me up, but I can't resist anything that's in the molten chocolate class. Bring it on," Jimmy said.

"You won't be disappointed, trust me. My wife practically existed on it when she was pregnant with our first."

Jimmy thought about it. *That would make a great article.*

Horace returned with the molten chocolate brownie and the check. He stayed long enough to validate that this was the best molten chocolate dessert, as Jimmy cut the brownie down the middle with his fork and went for the best first. The chocolate oozed out across the plate.

"Man, this is great!" They fist-bumped.

"I'll tell my wife another one joins the club!"

Jimmy finished, left a generous tip, grabbed the check and went to the register.

CHAPTER THREE

After a week of settling in at the apartment and work, Jimmy was getting to know the town and people. The books Divinia had given him helped in his understanding of the town structure and the leading families. The Diaz' were the oil barons, more specifically, Elizabeth Diaz, whom he assumed was in her 90s by now. She was the widow of Clemento, who built Clem's Corner as he was exploring oil and built quarters for his workforce. Clem's Corner grew from twenty-five small shacks and a general store to the town of 1,800 today.

The Stonerichs' had amassed their fortune from print media. The top men's and women's magazines in the nation, with spinoffs into other media over the years, brought the family back to their roots from the East Coast. The senior Stonerich, long gone, sold the magazines and established the first newspaper to support Twinkle and the surrounding towns. Sylvan followed in his grandfather's footsteps, and Danny had been born with a nose for print.

Inderpal Andrajula's family emigrated from India before the second World War. They brought with them spices from their home country and established one of the largest spice companies in the United States. Their storefront in Twinkle did a brisk business, as did their restaurant, the Brass Elephant.

"I'm definitely going to find that restaurant and store. I'm overdue for saag paneer and naan bread," Jimmy said as he continued to read about the families and area.

Trembo Jiltson cornered natural medicines all over the internet. Their smart marketing matched practically every known illness and disease with one or more of their products, guiding people away from prescriptions to natural remedies. They had a clinic in Twinkle that Jimmy noted, as he was vastly opposed to doctors who *practiced medicine* on people when all they did was write up RXs for drugs.

The Morales family of Twinkle, headed by Amelia Morales, made their money with booze, plain and simple. Tequila and Mexican beers brought in enough money to educate their children and grandchildren at the top universities, both in the US and Mexico.

By the time Jimmy finished reading about the families, he pondered whether he should resurrect his blog. Even though The Big City, with a population of 7.1 million, contained every type of commerce imaginable, his creativity had dried up. That had been the first sign that he was stuck, but he couldn't figure out what the problem was.

Now, as he reflected on his former life after only one week in the country town, which was 0.04 percent the size of the city where he was born, he thought he finally understood what had stifled him. Traffic jams. Absolutely no connection to neighbors —they were afraid to answer their doors. Noise pollution from vehicles, stereo systems, TVs, store and restaurant music— everywhere he went there was noise. The list went on and on. He was so happy to be gone from there.

He called Brian and brought him up to date. He and Brian McKinley had been best friends since they were five. Brian's hair stuck out in every direction, and Tommy Baker picked on him throughout elementary school. Jimmy stuck up for Brian, and by the time they got to middle school, he told Tommy that while Brian still had scarecrow hair, at least he didn't have acne that would leave scars. That ended Tommy's bullying.

Jimmy's latest assignment for the TIN was to cover the rumor that Bruce Wojkenski had prize-winning beefsteak tomatoes. Jimmy steered the CR-V in that direction, taking County Road 22 to the southern edge of the Twinkle Town boundary. After driving down CR 22 for a spell, he realized that what he saw on both sides of the road were rows upon rows of vegetable plants in various stages of growth.

Jimmy found the road leading up to the farm buildings and a house. It far surpassed what was considered a driveway with two distinct lanes. He pulled up in front of the large farmhouse, got out, and rang the doorbell. A middle-aged woman in a halter top, cargo shorts with pockets filled with various gardening tools, and hair on top of her head in a messy bun, answered the door. She had a suntanned face with just the beginning stages of wrinkles and cool, green eyes.

"Mrs. Wojkenski?" Jimmy asked. "I'm Jimmy Katz with the TIN, and I'd like to talk to you and your husband about your beefsteak tomatoes."

"Hi, Jimmy. Come in. I'll buzz Bruce," she said. "I'm Sharon."

He stepped into the house, and Sharon led him to the kitchen. The counters and table were overflowing with tomatoes in crates.

"I'm cleaning up some tomatoes for the farmers market," she explained.

"How many do you typically take with you?" he asked.

"Thirty or forty crates. We won't bring a single tomato home," she boasted with pride.

The kitchen door opened, and Bruce Wojkenski entered wearing coveralls. He was a big man without an ounce of fat on his body. A green cap with a large, embroidered "W" on the bill sat on his head, keeping his face shaded from the sun outside.

"Bruce, honey, this is Jimmy Katz with the paper," Sharon said. "I suspect he's a city boy and doesn't have experience with vegetable farms, so go easy on him." She winked at Jimmy.

Bruce shook Jimmy's hand.

"You're right. I just moved here a week ago," Jimmy said.

Bruce showed Jimmy around the farm. He learned that while the Wojkenski farm wasn't certified organic, they didn't use any pesticides, and there were no GMO crops within the county or surrounding areas. They used manure from local farms for fertilizer, and they rotated crops.

He went home with a load of produce and the biggest tomato he had ever seen. Jimmy went into Mrs. Potts' kitchen while balancing a crate of produce.

"What do you have there?" Mrs. Potts asked when she spied him. She noted ears of corn, a large bunch of celery, broccoli, summer squash, zucchini, and tomatoes.

"I was out at the Wojkenski farm for an article and they gave me a ton of produce," he explained.

"Doesn't your bird eat all of this?" she asked.

"Guppy has his own supply upstairs. I didn't want it to go to waste, so I'm sharing it with you," Jimmy said.

"The Wojkenski's have the best produce around. Do you know where the farmers market is downtown?" Mrs. Potts asked.

He shook his head, not recalling having passed it in his travels. "It's open Wednesdays from seven to seven over on Bunker Street," she explained. "There's a large parking lot, and rows of booths selling everything from produce to eggs, meats, beverages, craft things, jewelry—you get the picture."

"I'll have to check that out," Jimmy said. "I couldn't get over the size of the tomatoes. I have one upstairs that must be six inches in diameter. I can't wait to cut into it."

"You won't be disappointed," Mrs. Potts said. "Oh, when you trim your veggies and fruit, anything you don't want Guppy to have, toss out into the backyard for the birds and squirrels. Just make sure you chop them up into manageable pieces for the wildlife.

THREE PLEASANT MONTHS HAD PASSED. Jimmy found himself content with his new lifestyle. He and Mrs. Potts had a good working relationship. He no longer locked his apartment, as she was the designated bird watcher when he was gone. George and Jerry had completed the gazebo, which was larger than he expected, and Jimmy installed a fake tree for his bird.

As he carried a green plastic bowl of chopped rejected veggies and wilted fruit down the stairs and through the house to the back door, he noticed dark clouds moving in. He opened the door and stepped out, almost tripping over a tiny kitten on the bottom stair that appeared to be crying, but didn't emit any sound.

He tossed the contents of the bowl out onto the grass, set the bowl on a porch table and scooped up the kitten. Jimmy's eyes searched the yard and didn't see a mother cat or other kittens.

"Where did you come from, sweetheart? You're just a baby!" He stroked the champagne-colored back that promised a few stripes and dots and gently rubbed the top of the kitten's head. Brown ears, wide blue eyes, and tiger stripes adorned the head. A striped tail wrapped around champagne legs and one brown foot.

Jimmy brought the kitten into the house. "Mrs. Potts? Mrs. Potts!"

The landlady stuck her head out of the kitchen door as she wiped her hands on a dishtowel. "What's wrong? Is Guppy okay?" She saw the tiny bundle in Jimmy's hands. "Oh, my! Where did you find that kitten?"

"On the bottom step. It's not making any sound, but it's crying! I didn't see the mother anywhere," Jimmy said, somewhat distressed.

"It looks too young to be without a mother. You'd better get over to Doc Halliday's," Mrs. Potts said as she rubbed a finger down the kitten's back. "What a pretty little thing."

"I'd better call the TIN and let them know I'll be late," Jimmy said. He hurried through the house to the stairs and entered his apartment. "Look, Guppy. An abandoned kitten! I've got to go over to the vet's and have it checked out. I'm not sure if it's a boy or a girl."

Guppy walked along one of his branches and stopped within a few inches of Jimmy. "Girlfriend!"

"You think it's a girl?"

"My girlfriend!" the bird squawked loudly.

Jimmy set the kitten on the floor and pulled out his phone. "Milly, can you let Bill know I'm going to be late? I found an abandoned kitten and have to go see Doc Halliday."

He took a picture of the kitten and texted it to Milly. Then he went into his bedroom and opened the closet door. He grabbed a shoebox, removed the shoes, and went into the bathroom. He placed a hand towel in the box, then returned to the living room, scooped up the kitten and placed her in it. "Sweetheart, I'm taking you to the doc's so we can find out if someone reported you missing," Jimmy said. "Be back soon, Guppy."

"Return to me!" Guppy squawked.

JIMMY PULLED INTO THE PARKING LOT OF DOC Halliday's office. He heard dogs barking in the outdoor area in the back where the boarded dogs could play. Jimmy gathered up the shoebox and went inside.

"May I help you?" A badge identified the woman at the front desk as Iris Roonchester, who wore eyeglasses too large for her face.

"Hi. I found an abandoned kitten. Do you know if anyone is missing one?"

"Oh, my goodness! What a precious little thing!" Iris gushed. "Let's have the doc take a look at her. She looks to be around four weeks old, but I might be mistaken."

"You think it's a girl? My bird thought so too," Jimmy said.

"What kind of bird do you have?" she asked.

"Guppy's an Amazon parrot," he said.

"Why don't I have you fill out this card and I'll set up an account for you. That way, if you ever have to bring your bird in, we'll have the information."

He set the box on the counter and filled in all the pertinent details as Iris watched.

"You live at Mrs. Potts' boarding house?"

"Uh huh," he said while printing information on the card.

"I stayed over there for a couple of months when my husband and I went through a rough patch. We figured it out; our tenth anniversary is approaching. Everyone loves Mrs. Potts," she said.

Jimmy finished filling in Guppy's details, then slid the card across the counter to Iris. She snatched it up and clipped it to a file folder, then stood.

"Come on back." She led him through the door into an examination room. "The doc will be right with you."

Jimmy placed the shoebox on the stainless-steel table. The door opened, and Doc Halliday stepped into the room. He looked like he had stepped out of the Old West with his white vet coat over a long-sleeved shirt with a bolo tie, jeans, big belt buckle, and cowboy boots.

He reached out a hand and shook Jimmy's. "Doc Halliday. Good to meet you. What have we got here? Iris said you found a kitten." He saw the tiny bundle in the shoebox, reached in, picked it up and turned it over. "Looks like you've got a little girl. Can't be any more than five weeks old. Part Siamese and part tabby, I suspect."

"She doesn't seem to have a voice," Jimmy said, worried.

"Poor thing's traumatized from being separated from her mama and littermates," Doc Halliday said. He checked her over. "Going to have to feed her two to three times a day. Should be weaned, so that's less of a problem—you won't have to bottle-feed her. I can give you some kitten wet food and baby dry kibble to hold you over until you get over to the Dime Water store. Make sure you get a litter box and gravel. Don't get the clay gravel. That leads to kidney and bladder problems."

Doc Halliday walked Jimmy to the front and repeated the supply list to Iris. She grabbed a sample bag of baby kitten kibble and two small cans of wet food.

Jimmy paid the bill with his credit card, grabbed the plastic bag of supplies, and headed out the door. He gently set the shoebox on the passenger seat, then opened the back door and deposited the supplies. He slipped behind the steering wheel, started the CR-V, and glanced over at the kitten.

"Looks like I've adopted a kitten." He stroked the kitten's back. "How about if I call you Maddy. Do you like that name?"

Wide blue eyes gazed up at him adoringly. She squeaked out a tiny meow.

"Maddy it is then. Glad you like it. We're going to the store." He drove over to the Dime Water Foo(d) store and parked. He grabbed the shoebox and carried it into the store and set it in the child seat of the cart. He stopped a clerk and asked where the pet food section was and was pointed in the right direction.

The clerk noticed the kitten. "Oh, what a tiny little kitten!"

"Just came from the vet and have to get supplies. She was abandoned," Jimmy said.

"What's her name?" the clerk asked.

"Maddy."

Jimmy thanked the girl and pushed the cart through the store to the pet food section. He perused the shelves, found the baby kibble, wet food, bowls with fish on the bottom, a soft brush, and some toys. He looked over litter boxes. Some had sides that were too high for the kitten. He chose one for when Maddy was bigger, studied the litter and decided on World's Best.

He steered the cart over to the baking supplies section of the store and found a 9 x 13 x 2-inch cake pan with a lid that would work for Maddy's first litter box.

Jimmy headed to the front of the store, checked out amid oohs and awes from everyone who saw Maddy.

Jimmy finally made it home. He unlocked the front door, carried the shoebox upstairs along with a bag of supplies, and went back downstairs to get the rest of the loot.

"Okay, Guppy. I've named the kitten Maddy. Can you say Maddy?"

"Caddy."

"No, Maddy. Come on, say it with me. M.A.D.D.Y."

"Maddy!"

"That's it. I've got to set up her litter box and give her something to eat. She's probably starving."

"Food time!" Guppy hollered.

Jimmy washed the two white bowls. He filled one with

water and placed some dry kibble and a spoonful of wet food in a bowl and mixed it up. He placed the bowls against the wall, retrieved Maddy from the shoebox and showed her the food and water.

The kitten wobbled on weak legs to the dishes and managed to eat a little.

Jimmy washed the baking pan, dried it thoroughly and filled it with litter. He put it in the bathroom. Then he decided that was too far away for those tiny legs, so he decided to keep the pantry door open and place the litter box on the floor where it would be out of the way.

When Maddy finished eating, Jimmy picked her up and set her into the litter box. She understood the premise, scratched the litter and squatted.

"Good girl!" Jimmy boasted like a proud father. He brought her back to the living room and settled her into her shoebox. "Be right back."

Jimmy opened the door and clomped down the stairs. "Mrs. Potts?"

The landlady popped her head out of her bedroom door. "What'd the doc say?"

"She's a little girl, and I named her Maddy. He thinks she's approximately five weeks old and said she was most likely half Siamese and half tabby. I stopped at the Dime Water Foo and bought supplies."

"Why don't you show me where everything is," Mrs. Potts said.

"You're the best, Mrs. Potts! Back in The Big City, the apartment office would charge me two hundred bucks for a cat deposit, and I'd have to pay cat rent!"

She looked at him as if he were crazy. "Cat rent? You can't be making that up."

"I'm serious. Things have really changed for the worse. It

seems as if renters are treated like second-class citizens if they have pets. The last place I lived only charged me a seventy-five-dollar deposit because they didn't have any experience with birds, and I had to pay five dollars for pet rent."

They climbed the stairs. Maddy was asleep in her shoebox. Jimmy showed the landlady where the supplies were and explained how he'd move the litter box little by little as Maddy grew up so it would eventually end up in the bathroom.

"So, she needs both dry and wet food two to three times a day?" Mrs. Potts asked.

"Yeah. She just ate. Should I leave the rest of the food in her dish, or should I put it in the refrigerator?" he asked.

"I'd leave it. She might get hungry when she wakes up. I'll check on her in an hour or so," she said.

"I'd better get to work," Jimmy said. He grabbed his brief-case, walked over to Guppy's tree and rubbed the bird on the head and down his back. "See you later, Guppy. Take care of Maddy."

"Babysitter!" Guppy declared.

Jimmy and Mrs. Potts left the apartment.

CHAPTER FOUR

The front door of the TIN opened and a dishwater blonde charged in, her face a mask of pure venom.

"Hi, SueEllen," Milly said, the greeting tumbling out of her mouth. "What brings..."

The irate woman stormed through the newsroom zigzagging around desks, tables and waste baskets. She stepped over taped cords on the floor and made a beeline to Deuce's desk. He jumped to his feet.

"SueEllen! What are you doing here?" the sports reporter paled. He recognized the situation, being no stranger to a string of women he had pursued and dumped throughout the county.

"How dare you tell Marivelle that I was an insipid twit, and that you weren't seeing me anymore!" the flighty blonde practically screeched.

Eddie stood in the doorway of his office, phone in hand, recording the encounter.

"We DID break up, SueEllen," Deuce said with his hands on his hips. "It's none of your business who I talk to or what I say. Get over it."

Danny and Jimmy stared in wide-eyed wonder from their desks. The back door opened. Bill and Sylvan returned from lunch amid the lover's row.

"What's going on here?" Sylvan demanded.

"SueEllen was just leaving!" Deuce announced.

"We have not finished our business!" she declared.

Sylvan crossed the floor to the woman, put his hand on her elbow and steered her away from his sportswriter to the door. "Don't make me call your father, SueEllen. Haven't you embarrassed yourself enough by coming here and making a fool out of yourself?"

Her face went through several changes and ended up flushed bright pink with her eyes wide with knowing. "Sylvan, please don't call my daddy! I'm sorry I disrupted things and caused a scene. I swear it will never happen again." She glanced across the floor to Deuce and gave him piercing eyes of pure hatred. "That man is not worth the wrath of my daddy."

She turned and marched to the front door, exiting without another word.

Sylvan headed to his office, "Deuce!"

The sportswriter swallowed hard, followed the big boss into his office and closed the door behind him.

"Everyone back to work. Show's over," Bill said as he headed to his office. He spotted Eddie. "Did you get everything?"

Eddie Garcia chuckled. "You bet! I'll edit it down to a few choice clips and join them together."

"Poor Deuce," Milly said.

Danny wadded some paper and threw it Milly's way. "Deuce leaves a string of women behind him like the clutter from a tornado."

They couldn't quite make out all the words Sylvan was yelling, but the door finally opened and Deuce slinked back to his desk and tried to make himself invisible.

Everyone tried to avoid looking at him, but Jimmy's desk was situated so that he faced the sportswriter. Rumors about his star-crossed affairs had crossed his path, but he never thought much of them, given that he didn't personally know Deuce. Small towns thrived on a well-run rumor mill that started across back fences, were discussed in great detail at the diners and cafes, and blossomed exponentially.

Gert returned from an appointment, felt the tension in the

office and spotted everyone's eyes avoiding each other. "What did I miss?" she whispered to Milly.

"SueEllen erupted. It was like Mount Vesuvius blowing," Milly whispered back.

"Dang!" Gert shook her head, went to her office, and shut the door.

An hour later, Bill called across the floor for Jimmy to come to his office. He got up, wondering what was wrong. He entered the boss' office and sat in front of the large, scarred desk.

"Just wanted to let you know that your benefits will kick in next week, so you'll see the deductions on your paystub," Bill said.

A jumble of thoughts rushed through Jimmy's mind. He tried to recall how much money would be deducted for insurance and wondered if he needed a part-time job to make up the difference.

"Has it been ninety days already?" he asked, somewhat surprised.

"You're doing a great job. Sylvan and I are very happy that you joined the TIN staff, Jimmy. You'll find an increase in your pay next week," Bill said.

"Oh, wow! Thanks so much, Bill. I appreciate it!"

"We always start newcomers off at a low rate to see if they're going to stick around. Your writing far surpasses anyone we've had in a long time, so we want to make sure you're happy," Bill said. He opened a desk drawer, pulled out a box, and slid it across the desk to Jimmy. "Here's your new business cards."

Jimmy returned to his desk, elated. Maybe he could start a savings account, he thought. His old CR-V loan would finally be paid off next month, which would loosen up four-hundred dollars every month. He opened the box of business cards and pulled one out. He stared at his name and title: Staff Reporter.

MADDY CLIMBED OUT OF THE SHOEBOX AND LOOKED around. She spotted Guppy up in his tree. "Are you a bird?"

Guppy walked to the edge of the branch and looked down toward the kitten. "Yes. I'm an Amazon parrot."

Maddy looked around the living room. "Is this where you live?"

"This is where WE live," Guppy said. "You live here now, with me and our human, Jimmy. We call him Daddy—he takes care of us."

JIMMY WENT HOME WITH A SPRING IN HIS STEP AS HE climbed the stairs to his apartment. Guppy was squirrel-watching, and Maddy was sitting in front of the TV watching a children's program. She ran up to him, meowing a greeting as he shut the door.

Daddy's home! Look, Guppy, Daddy's home! Maddy exclaimed.

Guppy squawked loudly. *Now, every animal in a ten-tree area will know he's home. Keep it down, Maddy.*

Maddy turned her head toward the bird and hissed. That was the equivalent of someone sticking their tongue out, or spraying raspberries with their mouth.

Jimmy swooped her up in his arms and cuddled her. "How's daddy's little princess? Did you and Guppy have a good day?"

"Invaders!" Guppy declared.

"I trust you'll keep the invaders on the other side of the window. Would you two like to go out to the gazebo for a while?"

"Freedom!" the parrot belched out.

"Give me a minute to change my clothes." Jimmy headed to the bedroom with Maddy tagging along. He hung up his jacket, draped the tie over the doorknob, and emptied his pants pockets on the chest of drawers. Next, he removed his pants and grabbed the leg hems like his mother taught him, and strung them through a hanger, careful not to make any creases. He yanked off his socks, slipped into a pair of cargo shorts and a tank top, and dragged his flip-flops out from under the bed.

"Everybody ready for the gazebo express?" He grabbed a basket out of the pantry, shoved a dishtowel inside and folded one end back so he could prop a book and a bottle of beer against each other, then set the basket on the table. He reached down and scooped up Maddy and settled her in the basket. Jimmy draped a hand towel over his arm, walked over to Guppy's tree, and the bird climbed onto his arm.

"Gazebo express!" Guppy yelled.

Jimmy went down the stairs, through the house and out the back door to the gazebo. "Here you go, Guppy." The bird hopped onto his tree branch. "Maddy, are you ready to catch a few flies?" The kitten jumped out of the basket and leapt to the

wide ledge, her tail twitching as she watched squirrels leaping from branch to branch through the oak trees, and birds flittering around.

Once the animals were settled, Jimmy sat on one of the padded benches, leaned back and put his feet up. He opened the beer, chugged a mouthful, then grabbed the book, a riveting mystery by a well-known author. A lined index card held the place where he had left off a few days ago. As he settled in, his phone dinged a text.

Gigi: *Hi Jimmy. Want some company?*

He stared at the text and wondered what she wanted. *Sure.*

Do you know where I live?

Gigi: *Mrs. Potts' place, right?*

Jimmy: *Yes. I'm in the gazebo out back.*

Gigi: *See you soon.*

"Well, this is weird."

Barely five minutes later, Gigi was at the gazebo. He figured she must have contacted him from down the block or something.

"Invader!" Guppy squawked, broadcasting at his full range.

"Hi, Jimmy!" she gushed. "Wow, this is such a nice gazebo." She opened the door and stepped inside. "What a beautiful bird. He sure is loud. And this must be Maddy." She beelined to the ledge and stroked the kitten along her back.

Maddy had other ideas. She glared at Gigi, then hissed and whacked her hand. *My Daddy doesn't like you! Go away!*

"Maddy! What's wrong with you?" Jimmy said. He had never seen this behavior from his little princess, not even when Doc Halliday poked and prodded her. "Sorry, Gigi. I guess she's a one-man kitten. What brings you out my way?"

"I thought we could hang out, maybe go out to eat?"

Jimmy stared at the blonde bombshell, wondering where this interest had sprung from. "Listen, Gigi. You seem like a nice girl, but I make it a rule to never get involved with anyone I work with. My job is very important to me, and I won't risk my credibility, like Deuce seems to do on a steady basis. Sorry."

Gigi bristled. "Honestly, Jimmy. I'm not the office bimbo. I thought we could be friends."

"You've never even had a conversation with me at the office, then you show up here out of the blue. What am I supposed to think?" he stated, running the facts through his head.

Gigi stomped over to the door. "Looks like I wasted a trip!"

"I didn't invite you, Gigi! If you look at it from my point of view, you've invaded my privacy like some stalker. It may be the way country people do things—drop in without an invitation, but when it's a coworker that I barely know, that just seems too odd," he said.

She didn't even look back or comment. Gigi was out the door and tromping through the yard to the street.

"What the hell was that all about?"

He picked up the book again, but the moment had passed. There was no way he'd be able to sink into the story. Then his phone rang. He checked the name. Danny Stonerich.

"Hey, Danny. What's up?"

"Dude, if Gigi shows up, don't answer the door. I think she's having a hormonal meltdown or something," the reporter said.

Jimmy sat up straight. "She just left. What the hell?"

"She dropped in on Eddie first. Man, his girlfriend almost hit the roof," Danny said.

"Did Eddie say why she showed up there?" Jimmy asked.

"She gave some flimsy excuse about not knowing how to retrieve a photo from her phone. Then she texted me to go for coffee and showed up at my place. I didn't answer the door," Danny said.

"Should we talk to Bill or Sylvan about this? There must be something going on." Jimmy thought through scenarios. Nothing added up to anything he could figure out. "I wonder if something happened to her, you know, in her home life."

"The only thing I know is that she was dating this guy from Lockton for a couple of years and he got a job up in Dallas. He didn't ask her to go with him," Danny said.

Jimmy ran that through his head. "When did this happen?"

"Before you got here—four or five months ago. That's enough time to adjust, don't you think? I've been dumped before, but I haven't been in any long-term relationships," the reporter said.

"I think we should call the boss. Maybe she needs help," Jimmy said.

"I'll call my dad. He'll know what to do," Danny said.

"Call me back and let me know what's decided," Jimmy said.

The next day at work, Gigi wasn't in the office. Bill and Sylvan addressed everyone in the newsroom.

Sylvan appeared disturbed. He cleared his throat. "Gigi is taking a leave of absence to sort out some personal issues. We wish her well and hope she returns, but in the meantime, we will be one staff member short."

Everyone stared at Sylvan, wanting more information, but they could see none was forthcoming. Eddie, Danny and Jimmy exchanged questioning looks.

Bill took the floor. "Ag, I'd like you to take over Rimpole Diggelosky's new cookbook project. His first cookbook hit the Amazon Best Sellers list, so we will want to push this online with everything we've got. Eddie, can you check Gigi's computer and see if she had pictures of him, the cover, or a Word doc she had started? We don't want to have to backtrack if something is already in place."

"Sure thing," Eddie said.

"Danny, why don't you and Jimmy work on the city council, mayor's office, and police department news. You can divvy it up however you like," Bill said.

Bill and Sylvan went into Sylvan's office and closed the door. Everyone in the newsroom, including Milly at the front desk, shifted uncomfortably. Gert had a smug look on her face and was about to open her mouth when Milly puffed up.

"Gert, we know you had issues with Gigi, but you need to keep your opinions to yourself. You might want to dig down into your cold heart and find some compassion for that poor girl," Milly said with frost, before she turned her back on the room and focused on her desk.

Danny and Jimmy rolled their chairs to one of the tables. Danny got up, went to Gigi's desk and looked through her file folders in an organizer rack on her desk. He pulled three folders, then returned to the table.

"I can take the mayor's office," Danny said.

"I'd like the police beat," Jimmy said. He had always wanted to be a crime writer. He had worked alongside cops in The Big City while investigating his assignments.

"We can split the city council meetings," Danny suggested.

"Sounds good. I'll go introduce myself to the chief," Jimmy said.

"Whatever you do, don't ever call him Kenny. He'll deck you," Danny said. "Ask him to text or call you when something hits. That's what Gigi did."

Jimmy rolled back to his desk, grabbed his tie from a desk drawer and slipped it over his head. He tightened it, fixed his collar, stuffed a 3 x 5 notebook into his jacket pocket and headed out the door.

MADDY WATCHED THE CHILDREN'S PROGRAM ON THE TV with rapt attention. The teacher stood before a group of little children.

"Let's sing the alphabet song!" she said.

The children clapped and yelled "Yay," then they settled down and started singing. "A-b-c-d-e-f-g, h-i-j-k-l-m-n-o-p, q-r-s, t-u-v, w-x-y and z. Now I know my ABCs. Next time, won't you sing with me?"

Maddy hopped around her floor cushion, trying to sing

along. "A-b-c-d-f and g, h-i-j-k-lemon-p, cruisers, t-u-v, w-x-y and z."

Guppy squawked. "It's not f and g. It should be e-f-g. There's no lemons or cruisers. It should be l-m-n-o-p, then q-r-s."

"Oh." The kitten tried the song again while she hopped to each letter. After she finished the song correctly, she yawned widely, walked to her shoebox, climbed in and fell asleep.

THE POLICE DEPARTMENT was two blocks down Jiltson Way on the opposite side of the street. The freestanding building was built with brown and tan Mexican bricks over a two-foot-thick concrete structure. No one was going to spoon their way out of that jail.

Jimmy jogged up the front steps, opened the door and approached the front desk. A beefy sergeant in the tan shirt and brown pants uniform of the Twinkle Police stood ready for business. His name tag identified him as Sgt. Butch Gonzales. His belt included a Safariland 070 SSIII holster which held his Heckler & Koch HK45, a cellphone holder, and a spare ammo clip holder.

"You need to report an incident?" Sgt. Gonzales asked.

Jimmy pulled a business card out of the inside pocket of his jacket and presented it to the sergeant. "I'm Jimmy Katz with the TIN, and I'd like to introduce myself to the chief. I'm taking over for Gigi Thompson."

"What happened to Gigi?" the sergeant asked.

"She's on a leave of absence," Jimmy said, carefully. He didn't want to contribute any gossip about the woman, so he'd refer questions back to Sylvan and Bill.

Sergeant Gonzales picked up the phone and punched in a

number. "Chief, you busy? There's a new guy from the TIN here to see you." The cop nodded to Jimmy. "Go on back." He pointed to the chief's office.

Police Chief Kenton Price stood and walked around the desk with a swagger as Jimmy entered his office. Between fifty and sixty, the chief was at least six-foot-two, fit, and well-groomed.

The reporter held out his hand as he approached the police chief, and they shook.

"Chief Price, I'm Jimmy Katz with the TIN," he said.

"What exactly happened to Gigi?" the chief asked as he returned to sit in his chair.

Jimmy sat in front of the desk and fidgeted slightly. "She sort of had a nervous breakdown, but that's my opinion only. You might want to call Sylvan for more information."

"I never did like that Lockton guy she was with. Treated her like a rug," the Chief said.

"Relationships are tricky," Jimmy said. He hadn't had a steady girlfriend in a long time. The last one told him she couldn't compete with his writing career, which seemed to be more important than an intimate relationship. "Will you, or someone else, give me a heads-up when a crime or criminal mischief takes place? I'm not sure what the protocol is, and I don't want to annoy you."

"If you hear a siren, you follow it," Price said.

"What about when you're closing in on someone or something and there's no alert?"

"If we have time, we'll send you a text," the chief said with a grin.

Jimmy knew when the time was up. He handed the Chief a business card, then graciously said goodbye. He walked back to the office, detouring to the parking lot as he decided to go home for lunch instead of eating out.

CHAPTER FIVE

G uppy was napping when Jimmy opened the door to the apartment. Maddy was hunched on a pillow on the floor watching her children's program on TV. She jumped to her feet and bounded over to Jimmy's desk where he set his keys in a small bowl. She made a "breeeep" greeting and rubbed against his legs.

Hi, Daddy!

He bent and picked her up, causing her engine to fully engage. "Are you learning a lot watching TV?"

She meowed in the affirmative. *I know the alphabet song!*

Guppy stirred on his tree.

Jimmy fluffed Maddy's hair, set her on the desk and went to the refrigerator. He pulled out sandwich fixings and built a ham and cheese on wholegrain wheat bread, mayo, mustard, lettuce and a slice of the beefsteak tomato with stacker pickles. Then he cut it on the diagonal and pulled a plate out of a cabinet. He poured a glass of Mrs. Potts' lemonade and brought both to the desk and opened his laptop.

Maddy sniffed his lunch in anticipation of a taste, but was disappointed when nothing was forthcoming. She watched as he moved the mouse, pecked on keys, and a document opened on the monitor. She was more interested in this activity than she normally would be in snagging a bit of ham or cheese. The kitten reached out and touched the keyboard. A "Q" appeared on the screen.

Guppy! Look! I'm typing!

Maybe you could teach me, the bird squawked.

"Hey, no typing. Your feet are too big for the keyboard," Jimmy joked.

She sat and studied what he was doing as his fingers flew over the keyboard and words appeared on the white document on the screen. She recognized simple words she had learned from her TV program.

Jimmy tore off a little piece of ham and set it on the edge of his dish. He tapped the dish. "This is for you, sweetheart."

Maddy delicately snatched up the morsel and chewed, turning her head this way and that as her sharp teeth minced the ham. She then cleaned up with her pink tongue, making sure no telltale signs of ham or mayo were evident around her mouth or nose. *Oh, that was yummy!*

"I'm writing an article for my blog about an urban reporter transitioning to a country paper."

She made a noise that he swore sounded like "yep".

He typed a few more paragraphs, saved the file and closed it, then brought his dish and glass to the sink and rinsed them. Then he changed Guppy's water, pulled the bird vegetable and fruit bin out of the refrigerator and gave him a snack.

Jimmy grabbed his keys. "I'll see you two later. Stay out of trouble."

When he arrived at work, he found some type of radio device in the middle of his desk, along with a piece of paper with a frequency number. He picked it up and went in search of Bill. "Is this a police scanner?"

"Yes. Since you're covering the police beat, you'll need it. Make sure you use that frequency number. It's for Starlight County. You don't want to pick up Big-City police and fire calls," Bill said. "We don't have much activity in the big crime arena, but pick and choose the most interesting calls to chase down."

"Okay. This should be fun," Jimmy said. "Easier than

listening for sirens." He turned the device on, but nothing happened.

"Adjust the volume," Bill said.

Jimmy found the knob and turned it a little at a time, then a dialog sounded between two men. "How do I know this is the police? Could it be someone with a CB in their truck?"

"No, that frequency is only for our county law enforcement, so those are two cops talking about something."

Suddenly, a woman's voice came over the air. "Peterson, get over to the Armbruster's. Caleb is drunk again and smashing things."

"Roger that. I'm on my way."

Bill shook his head. "The town drunk. You'll hear that often."

Jimmy returned to his desk with his new toy, thought about it for a minute, then searched the Internet for an app. He found one he could download to his phone. He figured he could keep the police scanner in the car, but could use an app to alert him of activity in the sleepy town. Jimmy sent Bill an email and received a reply. His boss thought it was a good idea.

With scanner in hand, he left the office and drove over to the Biggem Diner where all the scuttlebutt happened over coffee and donuts. He was getting to know some of the locals. He found that the majority of people were friendly, but reserved if they didn't know you. Since he was a newcomer but worked for the TIN, he had an inch of a heads up over a complete stranger or tourist.

Biggem's was where all the working men gathered. It was a sea of ball caps in every color, with every type of slogan splashed across the bill. He went inside, looked around the room for an empty table and spotted Danny at a table for two, one chair vacant. He wove through tables and approached the reporter.

"Hey, can I join you? Doesn't look like there's any other table available," Jimmy said.

Danny pushed the empty chair out with his foot. "Has your name on it. What'cha been up to?"

"Met the chief of police, then Bill gave me the scanner, but I found an app for my phone," Jimmy said.

"Man, I thought Milly was going to deck Gert this morning," Danny said.

"How'd your father take it when you called him yesterday?"

"I think he suspected something funny was going on with Gigi, but when I told him about her visits to the three of us, he said he and Bill would handle it. They enlisted my mom to go talk to her." Danny shook his head. "I feel sorry for her and I hope she gets better, but she's spent the past few months dressing in revealing clothes and trying to grab onto anyone who'd have her."

"I thought that was the way she always dressed," Jimmy said.

The waitress showed up, and he ordered a coffee.

"No, she used to dress more conservatively. That guy must have done a number on her self-esteem. My mom enlisted Gigi's mother. She said it was tense. Evidently, her folks tried to convince her to move back home again when they saw she was unravelling, but she refused. Guess she's there now, though."

"That's too bad," Jimmy said.

They slurped coffee and sat quietly for a little while, listening to the conversations at the tables in close proximity.

"That damn dog got sprayed by a skunk. Second time this month!"

"Marian thought someone stole one of our sheets from the clothesline, but discovered one of our goats dragging it over to the barn."

"I found some new lures online. Going to try them out this weekend."

"Going into the bee business. We want to save as many honeybees as possible."

"Wojkenski's vegetables are the best. Have you tried those huge tomatoes?"

The waitress carried two coffee pots, one regular and one decaf. She went table-to-table, refilling cups and chatting with customers.

Jimmy and Danny left their tips on the table, then stood.

SYLVAN STONERICH PLAYED with the idea of a monthly magazine in full color. He cut and pasted a spread layout and tinkered with headings, fonts, and colors. *This would be good for the community.* He noted it for a catch-up meeting and was sad about Gigi because she would have been perfect to head up the project. He yelled out the door from his desk. "Hey, Bill... I've got a great idea."

Bill Trance walked into the office just as Sylvan's phone rang.

He answered it with his brisk *Sylvan Stonerich* voice. He immediately sat up straight, dragged a pad of paper in front and center, and picked up his pen when he recognized the voice.

"Afternoon, Betty," Sylvan said with eyebrows raised high. He made eye contact with Bill.

Betty Diaz? Bill mouthed his question while his eyebrows rose sky high.

Sylvan nodded. He motioned for Bill to step inside and close the door as he put the phone on speaker.

"Sylvan, who's this Jimmy Katz? Is he a new reporter?"

"Yes. Is there something wrong, Betty?" Sylvan hoped he wouldn't have to fire the reporter. He liked him a lot.

Bill plopped down into a chair in front of Sylvan's desk, a mask of worry plastered on his face. He shook his head as the thought of losing Jimmy swirled through his head.

"My great-nephew's name is Jimmy Katz. I want to know if this is the same boy."

Sylvan and Bill were on the brink of shock. Their reporter could very well be the heir to the Diaz fortune!

"Where's he from, Sylvan?"

Sylvan hurriedly clicked on his Finder and pulled up his HR folder. "He's from The Big City, Betty."

"Is his mother's name Evangeline? We called her Eva. My nephew was Errol Katz. They're both dead."

Sylvan quickly scanned through the application and other documents. "I'm not sure, Betty. There's nothing here that indicates who his parents were. There's no next of kin on the application, and no emergency contact—he named his bird Guppy..."

"You bring him over here so I can get a good look at him."

"When would you like ...?"

"Now! I'm aging here, Sylvan! If that's my great-nephew, it's imperative we connect."

"Sure thing, Betty. Let me see if he's returned to the office. As soon as I can find him, we'll come right over." Sylvan motioned for Bill to find Jimmy.

Bill was out of his chair and through the door in a split second. Gert was busy on the computer. Deuce was yacking sports on the phone. Milly's fingers clacked on her keyboard at the front command center. Eddie studied two monitors and moved data from one to the other. Ag, Danny and Jimmy weren't in the office.

Sylvan's door yanked open. "Did you find him?"

"Just sent a text," Bill said.

Sylvan pulled his phone out of his pocket. "Can't wait for a text!" He pulled up the reporter's name and clicked on his cell number. The call was answered on the second ring.

"Hi, Sylvan," Jimmy said. "What's up?"

"Where are you?" Sylvan asked, modulating his voice so he didn't sound like a demanding lunatic. "You need to get back to the office right now. It's an emergency."

"I'm pulling into the parking lot. What happened?"

"Just park and get in here!"

"What should we tell him?" Bill asked.

"We're going to have to punt. Don't say anything about the family connection, just that Betty wants to meet him," Sylvan said.

"That sounds lame," Bill said.

Before they could argue the point, the back door opened and Jimmy rushed inside.

"What happened?" he asked in a tense voice.

"The matriarch of Twinkle and Starlight County wants to meet you," Sylvan said.

"Mrs. Diaz?" Jimmy asked, gulping.

"Yes," Bill said.

"Did she object to one of my articles?" Jimmy asked, nervous. He envisioned filing for unemployment. He liked living in Twinkle and wouldn't consider moving back to The Big City, no matter what. But he wondered where he could possibly find work that equaled his job as a reporter.

"No. Evidently, she noticed someone new and just wants to meet you," Sylvan lied.

Jimmy let out a staggering breath he didn't realize he was holding. "Oh, I thought you were going to fire me."

"Heavens no. It's just that when Betty calls, which isn't often, we accommodate her, no matter how strange her requests may sound," Bill said.

"Let's go!" Sylvan said. "You too, Bill!"

The three men headed out the back door and piled into Sylvan's Mercedes. The car turned left onto Stonerich Boulevard, then drove right onto Diaz Circle, where Stonerich ended.

The huge house at the center of the circle was the Diaz mansion. The manicured lawn and lush landscaping were the envy of the citizens. Two other mansions were the only other structures on the street: the Jiltson and the Stonerich mansions, nowhere near as spectacular as the matriarch's.

Each house sat on five-acre lots, the richest real estate in town. While there was plenty of room for businesses on Diaz Circle, it was *understood* that there were no vacancies.

Sylvan steered the car into the circular driveway and parked. All three were keyed up about the impending visit. Jimmy opened his jacket and sniffed each underarm. He was relieved he didn't smell—that his deodorant held up under stress.

They exited the car and walked up the five steps to the front door. Bill rang the doorbell—it sounded like a temple gong reverberating throughout the house. A man in butler's livery answered the door and held it open.

"Hi, Jenkins," Sylvan said.

"Mrs. Diaz is expecting you," he said.

Sylvan, Jimmy, and Bill entered the house and followed the butler. Jimmy's eyes flitted everywhere, from antiques to crystal chandeliers to silver tea settings, artwork in lavish frames, statues, and enormous urns and vases. He had never before seen such opulence.

They were led into a conservatory—sort of an indoor garden—a room of floor to ceiling windows with lush tropical plants without a yellowed leaf among the jungle. Sitting in a high-backed, carved chair was a tiny woman of indeterminate age. Old, but not *old*. Sharp eyes that showed no sign of confusion. A superiority without a condescending mien about her.

"Hello, Betty," Sylvan and Bill said at the same time.

The tiny matriarch looked them over. "Good afternoon, Sylvan, Bill. Is this young Jimmy Katz?"

"Yes, ma'am," Sylvan said. His arm swept around Jimmy's shoulders and gently pulled him forward. "Jimmy, this is Elizabeth Diaz. Most everyone calls her Betty."

Jimmy stepped forward, hand outstretched. "It's nice to meet you, Mrs. Diaz."

She gripped his hand with surprising strength for someone ninety years old.

"Are you Eva and Errol's son?"

Surprised that this important woman would know his parents, he said, "Yes. When did you meet them? I don't recall ever coming to Twinkle unless it was when I was very little."

"Jimmy, I'm your great-aunt Betty Katz. We have a lot to discuss." She turned to Sylvan and Bill. "These are family matters. I promise to return your reporter a little later."

The door gong rang. A few moments later, three men were ushered into the room holding briefcases: Pete Daigle, Judson Diaz, and Godfrey Stonerich of the DDS law firm.

"Jenkins, show Sylvan and Bill out, please."

Jimmy looked like a deer about to be rammed by a pickup truck as the lawyers entered and his bosses exited.

CHAPTER SIX

A fter everyone was introduced and seated, not a moment was wasted.

"Jimmy, you're the last Katz," Betty said. "My only living heir. While there are Diaz' all over the town, county and the world, my husband's descendants are far and few between. There's fourth, fifth and six Diaz cousins, but no nieces or nephews. Clemento, my late husband, and I could not conceive."

The reporter was stunned into silence.

Three briefcases opened on the large, elaborate coffee table.

Pete Daigle produced a DNA swab and handed it to Jimmy. "We need to collect your DNA and establish the genetic connection, and also to preserve it in case of an accident for identification purposes."

Jimmy opened the container, carefully removed the swab stick, and stuck it in his cheek. After the requisite time, he removed the swab and placed it in the collection tube, closed it, and handed it back to Mr. Daigle.

The attorney placed a label on the tube. "Initial and date here." He pointed to the place with a pen. Jimmy initialed and dated the label. The tube disappeared into the briefcase.

Judson Diaz handed Jimmy some alcohol packets. "I'm going to collect your fingerprints. Wipe your fingers on one hand with the alcohol pad."

Jimmy commenced to tear open a packet and wiped his left-hand fingers.

Mr. Diaz removed an ink pad and a fingerprint card from

his briefcase and set them on the coffee table. He held Jimmy's left hand and maneuvered each finger separately on the pad, then rocked them onto the card.

Jimmy tore open another alcohol pad with his teeth and wiped the ink off his fingers. Then he used a new pad and cleaned the right-hand fingers, and the process was repeated. The card was placed in a plastic protector then stored in a thick manila envelope that disappeared into his briefcase, along with the pad.

Attorney Stonerich pulled a sheaf of 11 x 14 paper out of his briefcase.

Before the attorney began, Betty spoke up. "Jimmy, it's important for you to understand not only your inheritance, but your duty to the estate. We take care of our people—the citizens of Twinkle and Starlight County—as much as we can. Every day there are important decisions to make. When I'm gone, it will be up to you to carry on my legacy."

Jimmy was stunned. "I don't know what to say, Mrs. D... Aunt Betty. I remember my mother mentioning her Aunt Betty, but I assumed she... you were dead... er, passed away."

"Well, I'm still here, and hopefully I'll be around long enough to guide you," she said.

"Does this mean I have to quit my job? I love working for the TIN. I just got a raise..." He mentally floundered with
the family connection and all it meant. "Will I have to move?"

"Jimmy, honey, you don't have to make any changes you don't want to," Aunt Betty said. "Mrs. Potts is a good woman and runs a fine establishment. I expect if you want to keep working for the TIN, that's your prerogative, but you won't need the paycheck. Godfrey will explain all that when I shut up."

His shoulders dropped in relief. "I'm so glad to hear that.

Guppy loves his two windows and the gazebo—that's my Amazon parrot, and I have a kitten named Maddy. She's part Siamese and tabby." He knew he was rambling.

"I'll turn you over to Godfrey and the boys now. It's time for my massage. Come to dinner tomorrow evening," she said, and rose. "Seven o'clock. You may dress casually." Aunt Elizabeth (Betty) Katz-Diaz regally swept out of the room.

GODFREY STONERICH HAD a gentle voice and manner. The attorney was patient while presenting legal documents to the frayed heir to the Katz-Diaz empire, and requesting his initials or signature numerous times. Jimmy almost blanked out when he was presented with the net worth of the estate holdings. He counted nine zeros after the two digits. He had never, ever seen such a large number, and couldn't comprehend that he would ever personally be named in a document that declared it would someday be his.

Godfrey returned the documents to the manila envelope and slid another envelope across to Jimmy. "You might want to study these documents so you have a better understanding of the foundations and trusts. Be sure to keep them in a secure place."

Jimmy accepted the two credit cards: a black American Express Centurion card and a white Stratus Rewards Visa card. Each credit card had a hundred-thousand-dollar limit, which could be adjusted on a per-purchase basis. All his expenses would be paid by the estate.

Judson slid a checkbook bound in a leather case with the large letter K embossed on the front, across the table to him.

Mr. Daigle handed him a thick envelope. "Here's some pocket money. I'll take you to the bank this afternoon and introduce you to FeBe Morales, the bank president. She's going to personally oversee your checking account."

The lawyers stood. Jimmy stood. It was hard to realize that three hours had passed. It seemed as if someone else was controlling his body. He thought he was in shock and wished his parents were still alive to answer some questions. Now he understood how his college education had been paid for without student loans. The money had always been there for books, labs, and everything else needed for his education. He wondered why his parents hadn't informed him of the family wealth.

He didn't grow up with any reflection of influence. His parents had jobs. They lived a quiet life. Jimmy snapped out of his reminiscing when he heard his name. Mr. Daigle would drive him over to the bank.

Pete Daigle walked Jimmy through the front door of the Twinkle Bank and Trust on Stonerich Blvd. As he steered Jimmy to the corner office of the president, Divinia Reynolds, the librarian, waved.

"Hi, Pete! Hi, Jimmy," Divinia called out.

Pete waved back, then knocked on Ms. Morales' open doorframe. He and Jimmy entered when the woman stood.

"Welcome, Mr. Katz. Hi, Pete. Won't you sit down?" Ms. Morales said. She walked around her desk, closed the door, and returned to her chair. She was tall for a woman, at least five-eight, with blonde hair in a French twist, and young for a banker. He placed her in her late thirties, early forties at most.

Jimmy stared at the name sign. He had assumed her name was spelled the traditional Phoebe, but there it was in brass on wood as FeBe.

She noticed his interest in her name. "My name is Feona, spelled with an e, Beatrice. I've been called FeBe since kindergarten."

Jimmy stood, reached across the desk, and shook her hand. "Nice to meet you, Ms. Morales."

"Your checking account is set up. I just need you to sign the signature card. We want to make sure that there's no funny business with presented checks," she explained. "Wealthy people are always being bilked by shysters, and it's my job, as well as the employees of this bank, to make sure all our citizens are protected from fraud."

Jimmy signed the card.

"I'm sure the attorneys for the estate mentioned the quarterly meetings where we all get together and report to Mrs. Diaz. As the heir, you will also be included," FeBe said.

"We still have several things to go over," Pete said.

"I thought we went over everything in the meeting," Jimmy said.

"We figured you needed to decompress from the afternoon," Pete said. "One of us will call you tomorrow and set up a meeting."

Pete stood. Jimmy jumped to his feet.

"Thank you for... everything," Jimmy told the banker. "My pleasure, Mr. Katz."

Pete and Jimmy left the bank.

"Want me to drop you off at Mrs. Potts' place?" Pete asked.

"I need to get back to work. I've been gone for hours!" Jimmy said.

SYLVAN'S PHONE RANG. He answered it in his standard *Sylvan Stonerich* voice and recognized his cousin's voice. "Hey, Stoney."

"*Syl, listen, I know this is big news, but we'd like you to tone it down. Don't mention billions. Keep it to estate or fortune, okay?"*

"Stoney, everyone already knows the status of the Diaz..."

"About that. From now on use Katz-Diaz with a hyphen between them. People need to understand where Jimmy fits in. That he's not some upstart who weaseled his way into becoming an heir."

Sylvan quickly jotted notes on a yellow lined tablet.

"Better have Betty approve your news release. I'll look it over for any legal issues."

Sylvan steamed up a bit. "That sort of sounds like impinging on our freedom of speech, Stoney."

"Syl, think about it. We have a billionaire walking the streets. No one really knows him yet. Women are going to be showing up naked at Mrs. Potts' place trying to ensnare him. I can foresee situations cropping up," Godfrey said.

"I get it. I totally understand where you're coming from. I'll talk to Bill and the staff," he said.

"Okay. I've got to go." Stoney disconnected.

Sylvan was on his feet and out the door. He went to Bill's office and closed the door behind him. Bill was circling bloopers in newspapers—not theirs. It was a gleeful habit he couldn't break.

He looked up. "Uh oh. What's happened?"

Sylvan explained the situation about news coverage. "Okay. We've got time to scrap the current headline. Let's pull everyone in and have a meeting," Bill said.

Sylvan nodded.

Bill called the front desk. "Milly, call everyone in for an emergency meeting."

Milly sputtered. She wondered how many emergencies they could have in such a short time. She got busy calling and texting everyone.

The front door opened, and Jimmy entered.

"We're having an emergency meeting," Milly informed him. "I don't know what's happened!"

"I happened," he said. He shuffled across the room to the conference room and flopped into a chair.

"It's going to be okay, Jimmy," Sylvan said. "It will take some time to get used to, but everything will be okay."

"I can't figure out how I didn't know..."

"Families keep secrets, whether they want to or not. Sometimes bribed to stay quiet. It will be okay," Bill said.

Danny rushed into the room. "What happened?" He looked at his father, Bill, then at Jimmy. He noticed the reporter was off. Muddled. "Did Jimmy witness something awful?"

Sylvan motioned for Danny to sit. "Patience. Wait until the others get here."

Within the next few minutes, the entire staff was seated at the table, eyes on the big boss.

"Did something happen to Gigi?" Ag asked. "Has Mrs. Diaz..." Eddie asked.

"Are we being sued?" Gert asked.

Sylvan waved everyone to be quiet. He took a breath. "Mrs. Diaz has announced an heir."

There was excited chattering around the table until Bill stepped in.

"Please wait for the news," he said. "The Katz-Diaz estate..."

All eyes fell upon Jimmy. He was the only one in Twinkle with the last name of Katz.

Suddenly, the room erupted with congratulations and well wishes.

"People, settle down. We've got work to do, and we have to follow some legal tenets for the sake of Jimmy's safety," Sylvan said. He went on to explain what his cousin had said. "Okay, Bill. Take over."

"Eddie, take the current headline and shift it to page three. Danny, you interview Jimmy about his life in The Big City. Ag, I want you to write the lead story, being careful about the wording. From this point forward, the estate will be referred to as Katz-Diaz. Make sure the hyphen is always in there. Don't anyone refer to the fortune as billions. The DDS and Mrs. Diaz want to tone it down. I want to see all stories when you're finished. They're going to be scrutinized not only by Mrs. Diaz, but also by the legal team for the estate prior to publication."

"Now get going," Sylvan said.

JIMMY UNLOCKED THE FRONT DOOR OF MRS. POTTS' boarding house. He heard Guppy downstairs in the kitchen and headed that way. His landlady looked up, hurriedly wiped her hands on her apron, and rushed up to her tenant.

"Betty called me. Come sit down. I'll make you a cup of chamomile tea to settle your nerves," Mrs. Potts said.

Jimmy lowered himself into a chair. Maddy jumped in his lap, stretched up as if hugging him. Guppy, for once, was quiet.

Something is wrong with Daddy, Guppy!

"I never knew..." Jimmy said.

"Don't think too hard on it," Mrs. Potts said. "Your folks kept it a secret for a reason, and perhaps you'll find out why as time goes on. Betty Diaz is a good woman. We were all worried she'd leave her estate to some organizations or foundations and the money would leave Starlight County. Now, we don't have to worry about that... do we? You'll stay, won't you?"

"I love it here," Jimmy said. "I never thought I'd like living in a rural area, but the longer I'm here, the more I like it. People have real values here. The land, their businesses, the way the town is run. I've learned so much in such a short time. I lived all my life in The Big City and barely scratched the surface of what anyone thought was important."

"Your little kitty sure likes those children's programs," Mrs. Potts said. "She sits in rapt attention in front of the TV."

"Maybe Guppy can learn some new words," Jimmy said.

"He has a good vocabulary, although I hope he forgets some of the colorful language he learned from the sea captain."

"I've had to calm him down when he announces the squir-rels are invading us," the landlady said chuckling.

"He's convinced they're going to jump through the screens," Jimmy said, sipping tea. He reached for the honey and added a dollop to the steaming cup and stirred.

"I've made a pot roast with potatoes and carrots," Mrs. Potts said. "Why don't you have supper in so you can sort your thoughts."

"Thanks, Mrs. Potts. That sounds great. I haven't had a home-cooked meal since before my mom died," he said.

"Dinner will be ready in a couple of hours," she said.

A remembered thought brought panic to his face. "I just remembered, tomorrow night I have to go to the mansion and have dinner with my great-aunt!"

"Well, that's nice, Jimmy," Mrs. Potts said, turning to see the stricken look on his face. "What's wrong?"

"She said to dress casual. What exactly does that mean when a wealthy woman says that? Jean? Slacks? Should I wear a jacket? I don't have many clothes."

"I would think that means slacks and a polo, or a long-sleeved shirt minus the tie," Mrs. Potts said. "Why don't you call Sylvan or Bill?"

"Good idea," Jimmy said as he pulled his cellphone out of his pocket. Bill answered on the first ring.

"Is everything okay?" Bill asked.

Jimmy asked him to break down casual clothes so he could dress appropriately tomorrow night.

"Why don't you go over to Hector's and ask him to dress you?" Bill said.

"Hector's? Dress me?" Jimmy sputtered.

"Hector's Men's Store on Stonerich. He picks out the right colors for shirts, ties, styles that are flattering for your physique —all that stuff," Bill said. "I can call him and tell him you're coming so he can guide you."

"Oh, that sounds like a good idea. I'll head over there," Jimmy said as he ended the call.

"Hector will know what the best outfit to wear," Mrs. Potts said.

Jimmy fluffed Guppy's feathers, then stroked Maddy's back. "You two be good for Mrs. Potts. I'm going to find some new clothes."

"Dress up!" Guppy squawked.

Maddy gave an approving *mmrrpp* sound. *Have fun!*

CHAPTER SEVEN

Jimmy walked into the men's store and glanced to his right, left, then straight ahead. There were racks and racks of shirts, pants, suits, ties, shoes – everything any man would need to dress for success.

A young man sauntered over to him. "Can I help you?"

Another older man with a tape measure draped around his neck made a beeline to the front of the store. He waved the younger salesman away. "Mr. Katz? I'm Hector." The proprietor stood back and eyeballed Jimmy from head to toe. "Turn, please." He flicked a finger in a circle.

"Oh! I get it." Jimmy slowly turned in a circle.

Hector clapped his hands together. "Why don't you wait in a dressing room and I'll bring some options for you to try on so we can learn your preferences?"

He led Jimmy to the rear of the store where there were four open dressing room doors. Jimmy went into one. An upholstered bench was against the back wall, and hooks were on each wall waiting for clothing to be hung.

"Hang new things here, and rejects there. Put items you like on the door," Hector explained, pointing to the hooks. "I'll be back in a minute."

Hector swarmed through the racks. He grabbed slacks and casual pants, shirts in every color and shade imaginable. Hector browsed shoes but held off. He returned to the dressing room and hung the shirts on one hook and the pants on the other. The proprietor clasped his hands. "Try on an outfit and step outside so I can see if the sizes are right." Jimmy closed the door.

Jimmy slipped out of his clothes and set them on the bench. He tried on a pair of dark gray slacks, then chose a blue shirt that made his eyes stand out. He buttoned the shirt, tucked it in, slipped on his loafers and opened the dressing room door.

Hector appraised the outfit then tugged the sleeves. "Too long." Hector made Jimmy turn in a slow circle. "Pants work perfectly."

He ducked around his client, grabbed all the shirts and disappeared among the sea of racks. Moments later, he returned with the same colors in a different size.

Jimmy slipped into a blue shirt, and it fit perfectly, as if it were tailored just for him.

"Yes," Hector said. He pulled a small pair of scissors out of his pocket and snipped the tags off the shirt and pants. He grabbed Jimmy's old slacks from the bench and handed them over with two fingers as if they were contaminated. "Switch your wallet and personal items to your new slacks."

Jimmy transferred his keys, change, a 3 x 5 pad of paper, and a pen to the new slacks. He scooped up his old clothes.

"Let's look at shoes." As they moved across the store, Hector called out a string of numbers and colors to Jorge, his assistant. They arrived at the shoe department. Hector's eyes assessed Jimmy's shoes. "Size 12?"

"Yes."

Hector grabbed a pair of shoes. "Try these."

Jimmy sat in a chair, slipped his old shoes off, and slid his feet into the new shoes. The soft, black leather fit comfortably. He stood and walked around. "These are nice."

"Bruno Magli Maioco Cap-Toe Oxford. These will do nicely for now," Hector said.

They walked to the front of the store to a payment center. There were several shirts and three pairs of slacks hanging beside the counter.

Jimmy watched as Hector keyed in the sales. "Ninety-eight dollars for a pair of slacks? Fifty-six dollars for one shirt?" His mouth hung open when the shoes were keyed in: three-hundred-ninety-five dollars. "Oh My God. I should have gone over to the Wham-A-Rama!"

Hector stopped what he was doing. "You will never, ever set foot over the threshold of that store! You are a man of means, and the people in this community will look up to you! Your role has changed!"

Jimmy stared at the proprietor as his words sunk in. "I don't know how to live like this."

Hector patted his back. "You will adjust." He finished ringing up the sale.

It amounted to what Jimmy might spend on clothes for two years in his past life. He pulled his wallet out of his pocket and found one of the new credit cards and slid it across to Hector. His clothing was hung in suit bags, and his old clothes and shoes were dumped into a bag.

JIMMY HAULED HIS PURCHASES INTO MRS. POTTS' place. He followed his nose to the kitchen, where wonderful aromas assailed his senses. His landlady looked up and clasped her hands to her chest when she saw him.

"Oh, my! You look so well groomed! That Hector knows how to dress a man!"

"Do you know how much these clothes cost? Ninety-eight bucks for slacks and fifty-six dollars for this shirt, and almost four hundred bucks for the shoes!"

"Oh, he put you in low-end clothes and shoes," Mrs. Potts said.

"Low end? These are very expensive clothes!"

Mrs. Potts patted his arm. "Jimmy, those are probably the cheapest clothes Hector sells. He knew you would flip out if he brought out the big guns in men's fashions."

Jimmy flopped down into a chair, his suit bags dragging on the floor.

"Go hang up your clothes before they get all wrinkled," she advised.

He nodded, stood and climbed the stairs.

Maddy meowed approvingly, her face softening. *Daddy looks handsome, doesn't he, Guppy?*

Guppy whistled loud enough for the squirrels to scatter.

"We've got a lot of adjusting to do," Jimmy told his pets. He hung the new clothes in the bedroom closet. "Thank God he didn't sell me underwear. Who knows how much that would have cost!"

"Supper's ready," Mrs. Potts called upstairs.

"Be there as soon as I feed Guppy and Maddy." He went to the kitchen, pulled Guppy's bin and Maddy's canned food out of the refrigerator. He nuked Maddy's little bowl of wet food, added a scoop of kibble and placed it on the floor, then arranged Guppy's food on his plate and changed his water bowl.

He pulled on a pair of cargo shorts, a T-shirt and flip-flops and clomped down the stairs to the kitchen. "Do you think I can still wear clothes like this?"

Her eyes swept over his outfit. "You probably just need to upgrade."

Jimmy settled into a chair. The pot roast, gravy, carrots, and potatoes made his mouth water. "This looks wonderful, Mrs. Potts. Thanks so much for inviting me."

"You're welcome to eat here anytime you want, Jimmy. It's difficult cooking for one, but so much easier preparing meals for two or more," Mrs. Potts said.

After supper, Jimmy went upstairs and called Brian. "Guess what? You're not going to believe this in a million years, but my great-aunt Betty lives here!"

"I thought your mom said her aunt Betty died. Are you sure this woman is really your aunt?" Brian was a natural-born pessimist and always needed proof of anything.

"Bri, it's her!"

"Damn. She must be a hundred by now!"

"She's 90 and a pistol," Jimmy said. "Why don't you come for a visit? You'd love this town!"

THE NEXT MORNING, JIMMY DECIDED TO WALK TO the office. It wasn't far, and he needed to walk off some of his nervous energy. He wore his old clothes, figuring he'd save the new ones for important meetings. Along the way down Stonerich Boulevard, people waved at him. He waved back, wondering what was going on.

"Hello Mr. Katz. I hope your day is going well," a woman said as they passed each other on the sidewalk.

"Hi, Mr. Katz!" a man called out from his car.

He recognized the librarian heading his way. "Congratulations, Jimmy. If you ever need any help... you know, reference material, come directly to my office and I'll make sure you're on the right track."

"Thank you, Ms. Reynolds. You have a wonderful library," he said.

"It could be so much better with new programs and fixtures," she said. "Well, you have a good day now, you hear?"

Jimmy turned onto Jiltson Way, walked to the TIN front door and entered.

Words were spilling out of Milly's mouth. She handed him

a fistful of pink telephone message slips. "Everyone's been calling! The phones haven't stopped ringing, and it's just seven-thirty!"

She slapped a folded newspaper into his other hand and shooed him away from her command center as the phone lines lit up.

"Milly, put the phone system on night calls," Sylvan called out. "We'll let things die down and come up with a game plan."

"What's going on?" Jimmy asked.

Danny stood, grabbed the paper out of Jimmy's hand, opened it and held it up in front of him. Jimmy's picture was above the fold with KATZ-DIAZ HEIR FOUND.

"I wondered why people I didn't know greeted and waved at me," he said.

"What are you even doing here?" Danny asked. "You're rich. You don't need this job."

"I'm a journalist! What else am I supposed to do? Take up golf? Join the country club? Escort young women around like a male bimbo?"

Bill came out of his office. "Didn't you go to Hector's?"

"I figured I'd save those clothes for important..."

"You have a new image. Go home and change," Bill said.

"Is it really that important?" Jimmy asked, out of his element. "They're only clothes...very expensive clothes! I don't want to get them dirty before my dinner with great-aunt Betty."

"Did Hector only sell you one outfit?" Bill asked.

"Well, no..."

"For heaven's sake, kid, go change into your nice clothes," Bill said.

"Can someone drive me? I walked," Jimmy said.

Danny grabbed his keys. "Come on, let's go."

Bill walked into Sylvan's office. "He's got a poverty complex."

"I think he's just down to Earth. It'll smooth out as he gets used to the idea of being the heir," Sylvan said.

"How are we going to handle all these phone calls?" Bill asked.

"We'll listen to them, delete calls that don't pertain to news, and carry on as usual," Sylvan said.

Milly buzzed Sylvan's phone. He answered on speaker. "What's up?

"One of the messages is from a Big City paper. They want to send a news crew to interview Jimmy and Betty," Milly said.

"Forward all calls like that to DDS," Sylvan said. "They'll know how to handle those."

Milly clicked off.

"At least they didn't just show up," Bill said.

Gert popped out of her office. "My phone's been ringing off the hook with people buying ad space. "Jimmy Katz getting to know you" sales ads—some of the most ridiculous things you could imagine. How do you want to handle this?"

"It depends. Do they expect Jimmy to be there on the premises to greet people for their sales?"

"I can't imagine him standing by while Gunther pumps out a septic tank," Gert said.

Sylvan shook his head. "No, no, and no! You call Gunther back and tell him we're not selling him that ad. Use your common sense, Gert. We don't need a three-ring circus."

DANNY PULLED up to the curb and parked. He and Jimmy got out and went into the boarding house.

"Hi, Mrs. Potts," Danny said as he and Jimmy walked into the kitchen.

"Well, hello Danny Stonerich. What are you two up to?"

She looked Jimmy over. "Jimmy, why aren't you wearing your new clothes?"

Jimmy felt his neck and ears turning red. "The principal sent me home to change."

"Honey, you have an image to protect. It's time you took your new life into consideration," Mrs. Potts said gently.

"Yeah, that's what my dad and Bill said," Danny relayed. "Frankly, I don't see what difference it makes whether he wears new or old clothes."

"Well, young man, Jimmy's going to have young people... children... looking up to him as a role model. He can start by being dressed properly," the landlady said. "Would either of you like a piece of blueberry pie?"

They scarfed down the pie, Jimmy changed clothes and was scrutinized by Mrs. Potts, then they drove back to the newspaper in separate vehicles.

Bill popped out of his office. "Jimmy, DDS wants you to stop by the office this morning, but stop by Hector's to pick up your new suit before you go there."

"I didn't buy a new suit."

"I think your aunt called Hector," Bill said.

Jimmy stared at Bill for a moment. "Okay, I guess I need a new business suit. I don't recall DDS—is that the dentist? Oh, never mind. It's the attorneys. Where are they located?"

"At the end of Stonerich by Diaz Circle," Bill said. "You can't miss it."

He left the office and drove to Hector's. When he walked into the store, Hector and Jorge were all aflutter.

"I have a Canali Italian charcoal suit for you. I'll order more options when we see how this fits. I'm positive it will not require alterations," Hector explained.

They led Jimmy to the dressing room. Jorge hung the suit on the door hook.

Jimmy closed the door, slipped out of his dress slacks, carefully set them on the bench so they wouldn't wrinkle, and slipped the Canali pants on. They fit perfectly. He tucked the shirt in, zipped, then slipped the jacket off the hanger. It was comfortable. He slid into his shoes and opened the door for Hector's approval.

Hector and Jorge circled the heir. The proprietor slammed his hands together over his heart. "Perfect!"

Jimmy thought the man was going to cry.

Hector turned to Jorge. "Dress shirts! Ties! Socks!"

Jorge hurried away to do his boss' bidding. He returned with a white shirt, a red tie and gray dress socks.

"What's wrong with my socks?" Jimmy asked.

"You are not a Neanderthal. Those socks should be worn with sneakers. You cannot wear an Italian suit with socks that will stretch your shoes." Hector called out to Jorge. "Grab the black Gianni lace-up cap toe, size 12!"

Jorge returned with the shoes.

Hector relegated Jimmy back to the dressing room to change the shirt, put on the tie, and swap out his socks and shoes. When he was dressed, he was scrutinized by the clothiers. They both clapped excitedly.

"You were born for Italian clothes and shoes!" Hector said.

He handed Jimmy his slacks. "Personal belongings."

Jimmy pocketed his wallet, keys, pad of paper, pocket change, and a pen. He slid the belt out of the loops in the slacks and transferred it to the suit pants.

Jorge slipped the slacks and shirt onto hangers and rushed to the front of the store.

Hector manned the cash register. Shoes, $1,690. Suit, $1,795. Dress shirts, four at $150 each. Tie, $42. Socks, a dozen. Six gray, six black, $15 each.

Jimmy stared at the total on the cash register after the Texas sales tax was included as if he were looking down the barrel of a shotgun. He pulled the credit card out and handed it over.

"Don't worry, I will order an appropriate business suit, along with a tux this afternoon," Hector said.

"What's wrong with this suit? It's almost two grand! Do I really need a tux?" Jimmy sputtered.

Hector tut-tutted. "A man of your distinction needs appropriate clothing."

Jimmy took the suit bag and the shopping bag and left the store in a daze. He hung the suit bag on the backseat hanger, dropped the shopping bag on the floor and drove over to DDS.

CHAPTER EIGHT

J immy parked his car, got out and went inside the DDS office. The assistant walked him down a hallway into a conference room, while the partners exited their offices and followed.

Once everyone was seated around the table, the DDS partners sat with hands folded on the table.

Pete cleared his throat. "We hope you had a good night. We wanted to go over details regarding the estate. You appeared to be more than a little stunned at discovering your new relative and finding yourself as the heir to a fortune."

Jimmy nodded. "I'm surprised I got any sleep at all. When I went to the office this morning, they wondered why I was there. I can't just stop working. I love my job."

"There's no reason you can't write a column," Judson said.

By the time the meeting ended, he discovered that his great-aunt and late uncle owned almost every square inch of Twinkle, and the mineral rights of Starlight County. There were foundations, organizations, and corporations around the world in the Katz-Diaz empire.

He had assumed great-aunt Betty led a quiet life as a retired nonagenarian, but was surprised to discovered that she Zoomed board meetings at all hours of the day and night.

"Jimmy, it would be in your best interest to meet with us weekly until you get a handle on your responsibilities," Stoney said.

When he left the DDS, his head was filled with legal terms, corporate charts, and so much mumbo jumbo he had to sit in his car for a minute before driving.

He thought back to his childhood, college life, and early career. His parents had provided a comfortable home environment. Now, he thought about the tragic accident that took their lives almost two years ago. He had been in a fog through the following days and weeks. There were no out-of-pocket expenses. The family attorney handled everything. Jimmy assumed the insurance paid for everything. Now, however, he wondered.

The reporter drove back to the office. He didn't quite know what to do with himself, but he steered the car into the parking lot and sat there. He seemed to be doing a lot of blank sitting the past couple of days, but his mind was filled with questions.

Jimmy pulled out his cellphone and explored his contacts. He found the name he was searching for and called the office number. "Mr. Wilkinson, please, it's Jimmy Katz."

"Hello, Jimmy. It's good to hear from you," Mr. Wilkinson said.

"I thought I'd better let you know that I've moved and no longer live in The Big City," he explained.

"Oh, where did you move to? I need to update the file in case I have to contact you about your parents' estate."

"Well, I found a job at the Twinkle Independent News in Twinkle, Texas," Jimmy said. He waited for a response.

"You don't say? Twinkle? What an odd name for a town." The attorney tittered for a moment. *"How are you settling in? I never saw you living in a small town. Have you met any nice people? What's the population?"*

Jimmy pondered the attorney's response. It didn't seem as if Mr. Wilkinson knew about his new position in life. "I met my great-aunt Betty, Mr. Wilkinson. Did you know about her?"

"Your great aunt is still alive? My word! I assumed she had passed a while back because your mother always talked about her in the past tense," the old attorney said.

"She's very much alive and practically owns Starlight County and the town of Twinkle!" Jimmy said. They talked for a few more minutes, then Jimmy ended the call. He felt sure that his parents had not confided in the man.

"Why, Mom, why, Dad? What is this all about? Why the secrets? How come you made me and Mr. Wilkinson think that Great-Aunt Betty was dead?" He wondered if he would ever understand. There must have been some rift between his father and his aunt. He pondered how to approach this subject before or after dinner.

Jimmy went into the newspaper office.

Danny was the first to spot him. "Wooeee! Is that you, Jimmy?"

Bill and Sylvan popped out of their offices.

Jimmy's phone dinged with an incoming text. He saw it was from his great-aunt.

Wear your suit tonight. We will be Zooming.

"Looks like Hector dressed you again," Sylvan said. "Hector and Jorge know how to dress a man."

"I paid more for a dozen pairs of socks than I could ever possibly spend at the Wham-A-Rama in two years! Not to mention how much this suit and these shoes cost!"

Bill braced his hands on Jimmy's shoulders and looked him in the eyes. "Listen, son. You don't have to worry about price tags ever again."

"That's beside the point," Jimmy said. "It's excessive spending. There's not anything wrong with my old clothes. Why should I have to spend all this money on clothes? Who am I trying to impress? I don't have to impress anyone!"

Sylvan stepped up. "Chalk it up to making a little old lady happy, okay? Betty has lived with wealth and a certain sense of propriety for most of her life. Even Clem was clothed under her critical eye. It wasn't that she wanted to flaunt their influence; she wanted to establish a code for others to follow."

"Do you have anything I can work on?" Jimmy asked.

Bill thought about it. "Why don't you go see Chief Price? Find out if anything's going on around the county."

"Okay," Jimmy said. "Oh, and I guess I should mention, you don't have to pay me anymore. If you have to do something to keep it legal, just pay me one dollar a pay period." With that, he saluted with two fingers and was out the back door.

He walked into the police building. Sgt. Gonzales did a double-take. "You sure look different," the sergeant said.

"Clothes make the man," Jimmy quipped. "Is the Chief busy?"

"Go on back," Gonzales said.

Jimmy walked to the Chief's office and tapped on the door-frame. The Chief leaned back in his chair.

"Well, if it isn't the heir. Come on in, Jimmy."

"I thought I'd stop by to see if there were any situations on your books that I could follow up for the paper," Jimmy said.

Chief Price eyed him curiously. "You mean you're still going to write for the TIN?"

"Well, yeah. I need something to do, and I'm a journalist, after all."

The Chief sat straight and bored his eyes into Jimmy. "Listen, your new position puts a target on your back. You need to be diligent at all times, aware of your surroundings and the people within your vision. Even though we're a small country town, there's women who will flat out offer themselves up to you for a chance at your fortune."

Jimmy was quiet for a while. "I know. I've thought of nothing else. I wonder if I should grow a beard or a mustache to change my looks. The thing is, I can't live in fear that someone is out to get me."

"No, I understand that, but if you get the feeling that someone is watching you, they probably are. If you're in shadows, get into the light immediately. Do you have any fighting skills? Martial arts, boxing, wrestling?"

Jimmy shook his head.

"I'd advise you to get over to Moses Dojo and get in some self-defense classes. As the heir to the Katz-Diaz fortune, you have to be proactive, Jimmy."

"I'll check it out," the reporter said.

"Don't just check it out, get in a class, preferably private lessons!" Chief Price said with emphasis.

Jimmy left the police station and checked his watch. It was almost five o'clock. There was plenty of time to run by the dojo and talk to the proprietor. He got in the car and drove the three-quarters of a mile to Ruddy Duck Drive.

MOSES DIAZ, CLEM'S FOURTH COUSIN, TWICE removed, he liked to joke, was a compact man with normal musculature. Jimmy expected to see someone like Arnold Schwarzenegger, all beefed out, so he was surprised when he met the older man.

They went into Moses' office. "So, what would you like to learn?"

"Chief Price suggested I take private lessons for self-defense," Jimmy started.

Moses slapped his forehead. "Oh! You're Betty's heir! What do you know in the way of protecting yourself?"

"Nothing at all," Jimmy said.

"Not good. Leaves you completely vulnerable in case of a kidnapping attempt," Moses said. "When can you start? I'll teach you myself."

"I have to go to my great-aunt's tonight, but I'm free tomorrow," Jimmy said.

Moses perused his desk calendar. "Be here at nine-thirty tomorrow morning. We can work for an hour. Do you have any workout clothes?"

"Not really. I can stop at Wham-A-Rama and pick something up."

Moses stood, went to a cabinet, and pulled out two pieces of white clothing and a white belt. He handed them to Jimmy.

"We work barefooted," the instructor said. They shook hands, and Jimmy left.

JIMMY RANG THE DOORBELL AT THE MANSION. THE gong reverberated as if it were in a temple.

Jenkins answered the door. "Good evening, Mr. Katz. Come in. Mrs. Diaz is expecting you," the butler said.

"Hello, Mr. Jenkins," Jimmy said.

"Jenkins," the butler corrected.

Jimmy stared at the butler, not comprehending.

"Butlers aren't called Mister," Jenkins said.

"Oh!" Jimmy said.

Jenkins escorted Jimmy to a sitting room where Betty was on her cellphone.

"Mr. Katz," Jenkins announced.

Betty waved. "Divinia, I have to go. My great-nephew just arrived." She disconnected the call, pocketed her phone, and gently took his hand. "My, don't you look handsome. Just like your father!" She studied him in his new suit. "Hector needs to up his offerings."

"He said this was all he could do, but was ordering something better," Jimmy said. "Aunt Betty, honestly, I don't need these expensive clothes. I'd rather appear more down to Earth. Don't you think these clothes just alert someone to the fact I have money?"

Betty found a spot on the floor and studied it while she thought. "Jimmy, how about we strike a middle ground? When you are needed for a meeting, dress up. When you're out and about, dress down."

He let out a breath he hadn't realized he was holding. He had been worried about how his aunt would respond, but it was all for naught. She understood where he was coming from. "Thanks, Aunt Betty. Tomorrow I'm going to begin studying with Moses Diaz so I can protect myself."

"He's an excellent teacher. I, myself, hold a black belt in Tai Chi," Betty said. She stood in a defensive pose. "Moses gives me a refresher course once a year."

"I can't get over how different you are from any other woman your age," Jimmy said. "I interviewed some people in their nineties back in The Big City, and they were mostly bedridden in senior centers or nursing homes."

"When you keep your mind and body active, you won't fall into that trap. The problem with most people is that they retire, sit in front of the television and rot their brains. When the brain goes, the body falls apart."

She held her hand out. "Come, let's have dinner, then we'll go into my office and Zoom with the board of directors of the major Katz-Diaz foundation."

DINNER WAS SUPERB. THE ZOOM MEETING WENT smoothly. Jimmy thought it was going to be more mind-numbing mumbo jumbo like the DDS meeting, but it turned out to be a *getting to know you* meeting. He arrived home shortly after ten and found Mrs. Potts in her kitchen.

"Well, how did your day go?" she asked.

He gave the *Reader's Digest* version of the meetings. "Hopefully, you will have a good night's sleep," Mrs. Potts said.

Jimmy went upstairs and greeted Maddy. Guppy was in his sleep cage snoozing, so Jimmy didn't want to disturb him. He turned off the TV.

"I think you're watching way too much TV, Maddy. We should cut you back to only a couple of hours a day," he said. "TV can rot your brain."

But Daddy, I'm learning so much! She glared at him and made a *rrreppp* sound—it wasn't complementary.

Jimmy went down the hallway and entered his bedroom. He hung his clothes in the closet, grabbed his sleep pants, and crawled into bed. Some thoughts went through his head, but before long he fell into a deep sleep.

AT TWO-THIRTY IN THE MORNING, a sound woke Guppy. A ladder settled on the outside of the house. A dark figure stuck a short pry bar into the space between the screen and the open window frame. He yanked the screen away and climbed into the room.

Guppy screeched, "INVADERS! INVADERS!"

Maddy yowled and climbed up the invader's leg, her claws digging into the flesh under the pants. *The teacher said to call 9-1-1 in an emergency! Guppy! What should we do?*

Jimmy woke. He thought he was dreaming, then heard Guppy and Maddy. He turned on the light and was out of the bedroom and into the living room in a flash.

"I'm calling the police," Mrs. Potts yelled from downstairs.

Jimmy flipped on the kitchen light to see Maddy, claws sunk into someone's head, and that someone was screaming and trying to pry her loose.

"INVADERS!" Guppy squawked with all his might.

Jimmy grabbed an empty beer bottle off the kitchen counter and whacked the intruder on the back of the head. The man fell to his knees.

"Don't move, or you'll get it again," Jimmy said with force. "Maddy. Away!" He motioned with his hand.

Maddy retracted her claws and hopped to the floor. *Don't you move an inch!* She hissed at the stranger on the floor as sirens announced police cars racing down Stonerich and turning onto Burbridge. From the sound of it, every car on the force was on the way. They screeched to a stop in a haphazard pattern all over the street and on the front lawn of the boarding house.

Mrs. Potts stood at the open front door. "He's upstairs!"

Chief Price plowed into the house. "Stay in the kitchen, Mrs. Potts!"

Police spread out. Some went to the side of the house and discovered the ladder. Some went into the house and rushed upstairs. Others took to the backyard and the other side of the house, searching for any accomplices.

There was broken glass on the floor from the beer bottle. The chief came upon the scene while Jimmy approached the broken glass with a dustpan and brush.

"INVADERS!" Guppy screeched four times in a row. The Amazon parrot was wide-eyed at the rush of police entering the apartment.

"No! Don't touch anything! Can't contaminate the scene," the Chief said.

"Oh! Okay. I just didn't want my cat to get cut," Jimmy said as he backed away, leaned the broom against the kitchen door, then went to comfort his bird.

"It's okay, Guppy. The police are here."

"Cops! Call the cops!" the bird squawked, several decibels lower.

"Shh. The cops are here," Jimmy said as he ran his hands over the bird's feathers.

A deputy dragged the invader to his feet, and another deputy grabbed the other arm, cuffed him and held him.

The chief walked to the window, spotted the ladder. He stuck his head out of the window and called to the cops down below. "Tag that ladder." He pulled his head into the room and approached the perpetrator and grabbed the ski mask and pulled it off. He didn't recognize the man. Blood was running down his head from Maddy's attack.

Jimmy gasped and pointed. "That's the guy who robbed me at gunpoint at the gas station in The Big City! He stole my car, then torched it!"

"Are you positive?" the Chief asked.

"Wasn't wearing a mask. That face is etched in my head!" Jimmy said. "Maybe The Big-City police have his picture from the cameras."

"Do you have the case ID number? I'll call them and see what they came up with," Chief Price said. He turned to the criminal. "Who sent you?"

"Wouldn't you like to know?" the man said with a cruel smile.

The Chief patted down the perp and found his wallet. He pulled out a driver's license. "Reuben Brown."

CHAPTER NINE

Jimmy's head reeled with thoughts that the incident in The Big City wasn't random. Somehow, someone knew who he was before he was aware of the Katz-Diaz empire, or that he was the heir to the fortune.

He and Chief Price shared a look that said the chief was on the same wavelength. This robber being here was no coincidence. He had been sent by someone to do harm to, or kill Jimmy. They had to quickly unravel the circumstances and find out who thought they should be the heir.

"Take him away and book him," the Chief told his deputies. After the man was hauled out of the apartment, down the stairs and shoved into the back of a police car, the Chief turned to Jimmy.

"I want all the details about that robbery in The Big City," the Chief said.

"Chief, this was before I even considered getting out of The Big City. Before I discovered my great-aunt was still alive, let alone a billionaire," Jimmy said.

"Whoever it was, they messed up. The robbery at the gas station was staged as a warning, but it was ill-timed because you were unaware of your position here in Twinkle," Chief Price said. "I don't know if there's someone in Twinkle who's behind this, or someone from The Big City."

Since Twinkle was the county seat, one of the CSI officers was on the way over to dust the window sill and frame for fingerprints.

The sound of running footsteps up the walkway, onto the porch and up the stairs was heard. Then Sylvan, Bill, and Danny thundered into the living room.

"What happened?" Sylvan bellowed. He looked Jimmy over then the room in general. "You're not hurt?"

"No, Guppy raised the alarm, and Maddy attacked the intruder," Jimmy said.

Sylvan and Bill noticed the open window. Bill stuck his head out of the window and looked down. Ag was taking pictures.

"Let's go downstairs and see Mrs. Potts. She's most likely a wreck," Jimmy said. "Can I close the window?"

"It was open to begin with?" the chief asked.

"Yes."

"Go ahead. Don't touch the frame. Perp's fingerprints are most likely around the frame as he pulled himself into the room," Chief Price said. "CSI Lloyd should be here soon."

Jimmy closed the window, looked over the animals, then led the way downstairs to the kitchen.

Mrs. Potts had coffee brewing. "If it weren't for Guppy, things might have ended differently."

Everyone slumped into chairs. The doorbell rang.

"That's most likely Lloyd," the Chief said. He went to the door.

THE NEXT MORNING, Mrs. Potts retrieved the newspaper from the walkway. She opened it as she walked back to the house and up the stairs. The landlady stopped on the porch and read the glaring headline.

KATZ-DIAZ HEIR HOME BURGLARY FOILED BY

BIRD AND CAT, the Twinkle Independent News headline read. The story byline was by Danny Stonerich.

An attempted burglary plot on Jimmy Katz, the Katz-Diaz heir, occurred on Wednesday morning at 2:30 a.m. An Amazon parrot named Guppy, one of Katz' pets, alerted the household to an invader. The suspect, Reuben Brown, 32, allegedly accessed the second-story apartment with a ladder found in a toolshed. The intruder used a short crowbar to pry off the screen, then climbed into the apartment.
The parrot, with a very loud voice, woke the household of Mrs. Bertha Potts' boarding house. Mrs. Potts immediately called 9-1-1.
Maddy, Katz' kitten attacked the intruder. Katz disabled the intruder by hitting him on the back of the head with an empty beer bottle.
The suspect is in the custody of the Twinkle Police Depart-ment and is being questioned.

THE NEWSPAPER WAS SPREAD across the kitchen table. Mrs. Potts had finished reading all the articles when Jimmy entered the room, a haggard look on his face from a restless night following the harrowing incident.

"Sit down, I'll get you some coffee and breakfast," Mrs. Potts said as she slid the paper across the table to him. She busied herself with pouring a cup of coffee and preparing a plate of already-cooked bacon and eggs.

Jimmy stared at the headline, then at the photos. Pictures of Guppy, Maddy, Jimmy, and the sourpuss criminal were displayed in the newspaper. Smaller stories accompanied the main story that showcased information about Amazon parrots, Siamese cats with tabby bloodlines, and Jimmy's Big City, former job.

He slurped some coffee. "I should call Aunt Betty. She's most likely worried."

"Eat your breakfast first. You're low on energy," his landlady said.

"Okay," Jimmy said. He wanted to go back to bed and sleep the day away, but knew there would be multiple meetings.

His cellphone rang, but he didn't recognize the number.

"Jimmy? It's Moses. Listen, I know today isn't going to be the best day to start your training, so let's change it to tomorrow," Moses said.

"Thanks. I'm a walking zombie today. Tired and stressed, and I imagine I'll be in meetings most of the day," Jimmy said. "I'll see you tomorrow morning."

He no sooner ended the call when another call came in. It was the police chief. "Hi, Chief."

"Jimmy, your aunt wanted me to call you. We're going to have a meeting—you, me, your aunt, and DDS—in an hour."

"Where? At my aunt's place, or the DDS office?" he asked.

"This is police business, so come to the station," Chief Price said.

Jimmy scrunched his brows in thought. "Okay, I'll be there within the hour."

EVERYONE WAS CRAMMED INTO THE CHIEF'S office. The three DDS attorneys, Betty and Jimmy.

"All we know is the name on his ID, and we don't even know if that's his name, or an alias," the Chief said. "We're running his fingerprints and picture through the system to see if there's a hit from The Big City and beyond."

"Kenton, I know you're focusing on this being an attempt that started from The Big City, but it had to be orchestrated by someone from Twinkle," Betty said. "Someone thinks they will benefit from Jimmy's demise."

Pete Daigle pipped up. "Betty, with all due respect, before Jimmy entered the picture, you had bequeathed several local organizations, and various individuals. The rest would have been divided up among the Diaz clan—that's a lot of people the Chief would have to check out."

"Let's pull the Diaz chart and see if anyone stands out," Stoney said.

"That all sounds good, but who would have knowledge of Jimmy prior to him accepting the job at the TIN?" Chief Price said.

"Someone who subscribes to The Big City newspaper. Jimmy's name would be on every article he wrote, and someone put two and two together," Betty said.

"Until recently, you've only been using the Diaz name on all the corporate documents," Judson said. "This has to be someone who knew or remembered your name was Katz."

"Divinia Reynolds lent me some books about Twinkle, the first families, and the oil industry. I read the book that went into details about the town, and there was no mention of the Katz name. It was Diaz," Jimmy said. "So, it HAS to be someone close."

Not one person was happy hearing that information.

"I wonder why she didn't give you *The Katz-Diaz Empire*?" Stoney asked.

"Get me that Diaz chart ASAP," Chief Price said. He turned to Jimmy. "Are you starting with Moses today?"

"Tomorrow."

"It might be a good idea for you to have weapons training and a carry permit," the Chief said.

"I'll teach him myself," Betty said.

Jimmy's eyes swung over to his ninety-year-old great-aunt.

"Don't look so surprised, dear. I could shoot the legs off a grasshopper at ten feet. When I was a young woman, this part of Texas was still a wild, lawless frontier. It took a while for the people to become civilized," she said.

"Once you learn how to shoot, and not kill yourself, I want you to carry your weapon at all times," the Chief said. "Won't do you any good if it's in the glove box or somewhere out of reach."

"Okay. I guess I'll be able to protect myself before long," Jimmy said.

Chief Price stood, as did Betty and the DDS attorneys.

Jimmy stood. He was exhausted and just wanted to sleep. Betty patted his arm. "Go home and get some sleep."

JIMMY PLODDED UP THE FRONT STEPS, UNLOCKED THE door and headed to the kitchen. He found Mrs. Potts sitting at the table with a glass of iced tea in front of her, drifting off, staring out the window.

"Hi, Mrs. Potts. Is everything okay?"

"Goodness, you sure gave everyone a fright last night. Guppy and Maddy are heroes!" she said. "If it hadn't been for that bird yelling *invaders* so loud, who knows what would have happened!"

"My animals deserve a special treat, that's for sure," Jimmy said. "I'm going to lie down. I may not make supper."

"I'll keep your plate warm," she said. "My nephews replaced the screen."

"Thanks. Guppy appreciates a good screen when the weather's nice." He climbed the stairs to his apartment and let himself in. He slogged into the living room where Maddy was propped on her pillow watching a children's program. Guppy was quiet, sitting on his branch, watching the TV. Jimmy flopped on the sofa and watched the show on the screen.

There was fun and games about spelling and math. Another segment dealt with a computer and keyboard. His animals watched with rapt attention.

"I'm going to go lie down for a bit."

He plodded to his bedroom and face-planted on the bed. He was asleep before he could even think to remove his shoes.

WHEN HE WOKE, IT WAS DARK OUTSIDE, AND HE realized he was still in his suit and good shoes. He rolled to the edge of the bed, got up, undressed and slipped on cargo shorts and a T-shirt. Jimmy went to his little kitchen, flipped on the light switch, and pulled Guppy's fruit and veggie bin out of the refrigerator. He turned on a table lamp in the living room and went over to the tree.

Guppy's plate was empty. Jimmy brought the plate and water bowl to the kitchen, dumped out the water, and washed the bowl. He brought the water bowl back to the tree.

"Here you go, Guppy. I'm getting your supper right now."

Maddy was curled up sleeping on her pillow. Jimmy found the remote and turned the TV off. "You two are watching way too much television."

The kitten stretched and meowed in disagreement. *Guppy and I are learning!*

Jimmy returned to the kitchen and filled Guppy's plate. He poured seeds into the small accompanying bowl. After he had his bird all taken care of, he pulled Maddy's wet food can out of the refrigerator and heated a couple of spoonfuls for her little bowl, then added a small scoop of kibble and mixed it together.

"Maddy? You hungry?" He set the bowl on the floor, gave her fresh water, and checked the litter box. "I'm going downstairs for supper. Be back in a little while."

He lumbered down the stairs and followed his nose. "Do I smell lasagna?"

"There you are. Did you have a good nap?" Mrs. Potts asked.

"I needed that. Almost getting murdered is exhausting," he quipped as he pulled out a chair and sat.

"Guppy has been quiet today. I wonder if he's stressed about the break-in and all the officials in and out?" the landlady asked.

"Those two critters were watching children's educational programs on TV," Jimmy said.

Mrs. Potts placed a plate in front of Jimmy. "Here you go. There's more where that came from."

The doorbell rang, and Mrs. Potts rushed to answer it.

Danny followed her back to the kitchen.

"Hey, Jimmy," Danny said. He flopped a newspaper onto the table. "Didn't know if you had seen the paper, so I brought one."

"Have you eaten, Danny?" Mrs. Potts asked. "There's plenty."

"Well, since I was going to ask Jimmy to go out to eat with me, I'll take some of that lasagna," the reporter said. "Besides, everyone knows your homemade meals are better than a restaurant!"

Jimmy opened the paper to see the full front page. There was a great picture of Guppy, Maddy too. "The pictures came out great."

"At least the news happened on our schedule," Danny said. "Dad said they would have printed a special edition."

"It's been nonstop on the radio," Mrs. Potts said.

"Anything new to report?" Danny asked, always in reporter mode.

"Nothing I can talk about," Jimmy said. "You'll have to talk to the Chief and see what he wants the public to know. I'm starting private lessons with Moses tomorrow, and get this... my great-aunt is going to give me shooting lessons!"

"Your great-aunt Betty is nothing to sneeze at," Mrs. Potts said. "Wait until you see her in action. She used to take all the shooting prizes at the county fair but stopped competing to give others a chance at the title. She may be ninety, but you'd never know it when you see her reflexes on the range."

Jimmy grinned. "I'm looking forward to it. I never felt the need to take either of these lessons, even in The Big City, but now I realize that I've got to be able to defend myself, my animals, and you, Mrs. Potts."

After eating, Danny stood. "Well, I've got to get going. Thanks so much, Mrs. Potts. It was delicious. Good luck with the lessons, Jimmy. Moses is the best."

Jimmy walked Danny to the door, and they fist-bumped goodbye. He returned to the kitchen. "Can I help you with anything, Mrs. Potts?"

"Thanks, hon, but that's why they invented dishwashers. I appreciate the offer, though."

"I'm going upstairs to read for a spell," he said.

JIMMY HEADED TO THE SOFA BUT STOPPED AT HIS desk. He sank into the chair, grabbed the mouse, and woke his laptop. A Word document was on the screen. He knew for a fact that he had not opened any documents. He hadn't used his personal laptop in a while.

He leaned in and looked at the two things on the screen: cat and brd.

The hair stood up on his arms. Someone had been in his apartment! He carefully pushed away from the desk, retraced his steps and went downstairs and flew into the kitchen, breathy.

"Mrs. Potts, by any chance, did you use my laptop?"

She looked at him as if he had lost it. "Now, Jimmy, why would I use your laptop when I have one of my own?"

"If it wasn't you, then someone was upstairs!" Jimmy said, bordering on a panic attack. *What next? Wasn't last night enough?*

He pulled out his cellphone and called the direct number for the Police Chief. "Chief, someone's been upstairs!"

"Is something missing? Out of place? Explain! I'm on my way," the Chief said.

"I haven't used my laptop in days, but when I moved the mouse and woke it, there was a Word doc opened and there's something written on it."

"The perp left a message? What does it say?"

"It's odd. Someone typed *cat* and *brd*, which I think means bird," Jimmy said.

"The animals are okay?"

"Yes."

Jimmy and Mrs. Potts heard a car door slam shut. They walked to the front door. Sure enough, Chief Price had arrived.

CHAPTER TEN

"I hope I didn't mess up by touching my mouse," Jimmy said. "Did you open the laptop, or had it already been open?" the chief asked.

"It was open, and I don't recall it being closed before," Jimmy said.

The men went up the stairs followed by Mrs. Potts.

They leaned over the desk to better see the laptop screen.

Cat was on one line followed by *brd*.

"Do you think someone is threatening Guppy and Maddy?" Mrs. Potts asked.

"Their pictures were in the paper," Chief Price said. He turned to the landlady. "Need to get a locksmith out here on the double. Have all the locks changed. Who knows where the old keys are?"

"Oh! I hadn't even thought of that since that man climbed in the window," Mrs. Potts said.

"Are there any other boarders here besides Jimmy?" the chief asked.

"No, Mr. Mellany's daughter moved him to her house in Derrick. She was worried about him being on his own," Mrs. Potts said.

"Let me do a thorough screening on any new boarders," the chief said. He turned to Jimmy. "Don't use the laptop for now. I'll send CSI Lloyd to check it for fingerprints."

Chief Price and Mrs. Potts left Jimmy to contemplate the latest bizarre incident. He flopped down on the sofa. Maddy hopped up and settled in his lap. Her engine started, and the purring softened his stress.

Jimmy looked over at Guppy on his tree perch. "You okay, Guppy? You're awfully quiet."

The Amazon parrot did a little dance on his branch while saying, *cat, bird, cat, bird, cat, bird.*

Jimmy watched and listened, smiling at the little swaying dance his bird performed while talking. Suddenly, he sat ramrod straight as if hearing those two words for the first time.

"Cat, bird," Jimmy said. "Did one of you figure out how to use the computer?"

Maddy gazed up at him with a beatific expression and jumped to the floor, and studiously groomed herself.

Jimmy studied her face. "Did you? No! It isn't possible!"

He stood, walked to the desk and looked down at everything on the desktop without touching anything: laptop, mousepad, mouse, pen and small pad of paper on the mousepad, a chewed, unsharpened pencil.

"Where'd this pencil come from?" He pulled open a side drawer. His yellow No. 2 pencils were scattered among pens, three different types of erasers (pencil-tops, fat blocks, and sticks). He wanted to pick it up but had to wait for the police crime scene guy to arrive.

"Maddy, did you do this?" He stared at his little princess of a kitten.

She blinked with a serene expression on her face. *It's a secret!*

He picked up his cellphone and was about to call the Chief but stopped. "There's no way he'd ever believe this. I'm not sure if I even believe this."

The doorbell rang. He heard Mrs. Potts at the door, then footsteps coming up the stairs. There was a tap on the doorframe, and Jimmy recognized the same CSI officer who dusted for fingerprints on the window frame. The name on his uniform read Lloyd.

"Hey," Jimmy said. "Looks like this is becoming a habit."

"Not to worry. Someone is messing with you, and we'll find out who and put a stop to it," Lloyd said. He set his bag on the floor and pulled out a flashlight. He aimed the blue light at different parts of the chair and lifted several fingerprints with tape.

"Probably all my fingerprints," Jimmy said.

"We'll see," Lloyd said. He shone the light along the edge of the desk, the surface, the laptop, mouse and mousepad. He captured dozens of fingerprints. The officer then shone the light on the pencil. "This is a bad habit. Did you know that you could fracture a tooth by chewing on a pencil?"

Jimmy buttoned his lips. It was best not to blurt out the wrong thing, given that he suspected his kitten of knowing how to communicate via his laptop.

Lloyd finished up. "I'll run the prints. The chief will let you know what shows up besides your prints."

"Okay, thanks, man," Jimmy said as CSI Lloyd clomped down the stairs and out the front door. He turned to his desk. "Glad he didn't use that fingerprinting dust. That would have been a mess."

He sat at his desk, opened Safari and hunted for what he required: spy cameras and motion detectors. He found several nanny-cams that looked like they would do the trick. He ordered two nanny-cams and two motion detectors, thought for a moment, and had them sent overnight. "Screw the delivery cost. This is pretty important."

Mrs. Potts stood at the bottom of the stairs and hollered up. "Would you like some custard?"

"You bet!" Jimmy went downstairs to the kitchen.

"The boys will be here first thing in the morning to change the locks. They'll key all the locks the same so we don't have multiple keys for multiple door locks," Mrs. Potts said, shaking her head. "You just can't seem to get a break, Jimmy."

He wanted to confide in her and Chief Price, but until he had absolute, irrefutable proof of his suspicions, it was best to shut up and keep his thoughts to himself.

"Don't worry, things will be okay."

He enjoyed two custard cups before heading upstairs. He shut the door to his apartment.

"Okay, guys, I'm still pretty tired. Let's get some sleep, okay?" He ruffled the fur on Maddy's back and rubbed his hand down Guppy's head, neck, and back. "I'll see you in the morning."

JIMMY SLEPT SOUNDLY. When he finally woke, he heard a drill downstairs. He figured Mrs. Potts' nephews were changing locks. He washed up, combed his hair, pulled his clothes on and clomped down the stairs. Jerry was at the front door, and George at the kitchen door.

"Morning, Mrs. Potts. Will they be changing my door lock?"

"Yes, but that will be a different key," she said.

Jimmy pulled his keyring out of his pants pocket and sat at the kitchen table. He twirled the keys around, removing the house keys. "Here's the old keys."

"How about some French toast this morning?"

Syrup was already on the table. A covered plate was on the counter. Mrs. Potts served up three slices on a dish and handed it to Jimmy.

"Thanks. I love French toast." He slathered butter on the slices and poured a small amount of syrup between the slices and over the top. Then he dug in and ate with relish. "This morning I'll be over at the dojo for about an hour."

HE ARRIVED AT THE DOJO DRESSED IN THE WHITE uniform and only flip-flops since Moses mentioned they would be working barefoot. The instructor brought him to a back room so they would not be disturbed by the class that would be starting soon.

"Okay, are you ready to defend yourself?" Moses asked.

"I should have taken lessons a long time ago, but I'm here now," Jimmy said.

"You're getting the accelerated learning curve, Jimmy. We need you to be able to take someone down at a moment's notice. Betty gave me the details of the attacks. If the guy had been a professional, we wouldn't be having this conversation, or this lesson," Moses said.

They spent the better part of the hour going through basic moves, then moved on to more dramatic ones. After ninety minutes, Jimmy limped out to his vehicle. He ached from top to bottom. All those unused muscles waking up to a new day of being used. Even his toes hurt when he slipped into his flip-flops.

He drove home and managed to climb the steps to the front door. He rang the doorbell because he didn't have a set of the new

keys. Mrs. Potts let him in and noticed his stiffness as he crossed the threshold.

"A package came for you. I put it on your kitchen table. Why don't you soak in some Epsom salt?" she suggested.

"Do you have some, or should I run to the store?" he asked.

"Stay right here, and I'll go get the bag." Mrs. Potts

returned with a bag of Epsom salts. "I hope this makes you feel better. You want to loosen up those stiff muscles before you get too comfortable on the sofa. Otherwise, you're going to be very sore."

"At least I'll smell good," he said, noting the *lavender scented* on the bag.

"Don't worry, everyone loves the smell of lavender," she joked.

He climbed the stairs and opened the door to his place. "Who's there?" Guppy called out.

"Daddy's home!" Jimmy said.

Maddy ran up to him. She sniffed the white pant legs, then his flip-flops, purring and rubbing against his legs.

"I'm glad you approve. I've begun self-defense lessons, Maddy. Daddy has to protect you, Guppy, Mrs. Potts and myself from mysterious murderers, kidnappers and whatnot, but it sure hurts! I'm going to soak in the tub."

He stumbled into the bathroom, put the plug into place, then turned on the hot water. Jimmy dumped a good portion of the bag into the tub, then tested the water. "Yikes! Way too hot!" He adjusted the faucet, adding cold water.

He pulled a towel and a washcloth out of the linen closet, undressed, and stepped into the water. It was just right. He relaxed against the curve of the claw-footed tub as the water poured in. Jimmy sat up, twirled his hands in the tub to dissolve the salt, then leaned back again.

When the water reached mid-chest, he turned the faucets off. Maddy hopped up onto the ledge on the wall and sniffed.

Oooh! That smells nice!

"That's lavender you smell," Jimmy said. "It's an herb."

Maddy went about grooming herself. *I'll take a bath too!*

After almost fifteen minutes, Jimmy stepped out of the tub. His feet felt good, not to mention his legs. There wasn't any stiffness. He dried off, slipped into his briefs, then pulled on his cargo pants and sauntered into the kitchen. He opened the box, inspected the cameras and motion detectors, and made a note of what tools were required. A drill and a screwdriver.

He slipped on a tank top and his flip-flops and went downstairs.

"Hey, Mrs. Potts, can I borrow a drill, a screwdriver and a stepladder?"

"Sure. I keep those handy." She went to the pantry and retrieved her toolkit, and the Black and Decker drill on the floor beside it.

"The stepladder is in the closet in the hall. What're you doing up there?"

"Installing motion detectors at both windows," Jimmy said.

He didn't want to tell her about the cameras quite yet.

"Oh, good idea!"

He picked up the toolkit, drill, stopped at the hall closet and grabbed the step ladder. He hauled everything upstairs and went to work.

"Nobody is going to get in here without our knowing ahead of time," he told Guppy and Maddy. He went about installing the motion detectors at both living room windows, then thought about where to install the cameras. He decided one should point at the desk from behind, two feet away, and the other should be at a different angle to watch the keyboard.

When he was finished, he downloaded the software and installed it, then made sure everything worked properly. So far, there had not been any more messages on the computer. He hoped it wasn't a one-off thing.

Jimmy returned the tools and ladder, changed his clothes and thought about his day. He was going to stop by the newspaper to see what was going on. Then he'd stop by the police station for updates before going to his aunt's to see what was new.

"You two stay out of trouble," Jimmy said.

Maddy was sitting on her cushion, glaring at the black TV while grumbling. *How come we can't watch TV?* She looked over her shoulder to Guppy. *You're not helping. Tell Daddy we want to watch TV!*

Pipe down! Guppy said. The bird squawked loudly, then "TV's off!"

Jimmy sighed. "Okay, you win. Maybe you're learning more than I think you possibly could." He found the remote and clicked the TV on and adjusted the volume so it wasn't too loud. "I'm making the rounds today so I'll be back in a couple of hours."

"See ya later," Guppy called out.

Maddy squeaked out a tiny meow. *Thank you, Daddy!*

Jimmy thought it was a little too innocent and was glad he had installed the cameras. Hopefully, she wouldn't know what they were for.

He shook his head at that thought, left the apartment and the boarding house.

CHAPTER ELEVEN

Jimmy entered the newspaper back door. Ag and Eddie were busy with whatever they were doing, and Milly manned the front. He stopped at Bill's door, but he wasn't in. He went further down the hall, but Sylvan's door was closed and it sounded like he was in a meeting.

He wondered what he should do. It's not like he was on top of anything these days, due to all the activity with the chaos surrounding his new position in life. He walked to the front desk.

"Hey, Milly. Any juicy story tips come in that I could cover?"

"Oh, hi Jimmy. Not really, but you've had approximately..." she looked at a piece of paper where she had lines crossed off. She counted silently. "Let's see, you've had 23 marriage proposals today from all over the county and beyond."

"You're joking, right?"

"See here?" She showed him her scorecard.

"People are crazy! Why would any of these women think I'd be interested in anyone who called the paper and begged me to call them?"

Sylvan's door opened, and Bill stepped out. "Hi, Jimmy, we were just talking about you."

Jimmy walked to the back of the room. "Milly said all these women are calling..."

Sylvan appeared in the doorway. "Yeah, about that... do not call any of them back."

Jimmy gave the men a wide-eyed look that said he couldn't

believe what he just heard. "Seriously? There's no way I'd ever consider calling any of them!"

"We know that," Bill said. He had a goofy smile on his face.

"Do you have any stories I should cover?" Jimmy asked. "I feel a little guilty that I've been unavailable, and Gigi's on leave."

"Bill and I are quite capable of picking up the slack," Sylvan said. "We're newspaper men, after all."

"What are you doing today?" Bill asked.

"I had my first session with Moses and had to soak in the tub with Epsom salts," Jimmy said. "I've got to stop by Chief Price's office, then go see my aunt." He looked over at his spotless desk. "Should I clear out my desk?"

"Jimmy, we've got plenty of desks and tables if anyone new should start," Bill said, sweeping his eyes around the newsroom.

"Okay. I'll catch up with you later," Jimmy said, then scooted out the door and drove over to the police station.

He waved at Sgt. Gonzales as he skirted the front desk and continued on to the Chief's office. Jimmy tapped on the open doorframe. Police Chief Price looked up from pecking at the keyboard and mumbling to himself.

"Hey! Help me for a minute. I can't figure out why this report is so screwed up," the chief said.

Jimmy walked behind the Chief's chair and bent over his shoulder. "Let me use the mouse for a minute. Pay attention to what I do, Okay?"

"Okay."

Jimmy moved the cursor up to the Word document's Ruler. He used the cursor to point out the problem. "See all these marks up here? You've got tabs set all over the place. That's why your document's a mess." He grabbed the mouse and flicked several tab settings into oblivion. The document reformatted to an almost readable report.

"I can teach you how to set this up so your reports are all formatted correctly," he said. "Is this a template you use to make all your reports?"

"Yeah, I just rename it each time," the chief said.

Jimmy spent the next ten minutes showing the chief how to use Styles to create his report.

"Dang, you're good at this stuff."

"Well, I learned all this in J-school and at work in The Big City," Jimmy said.

"You could have a lucrative side business straightening out every businessperson in the entire county," the chief said, and he wasn't joking.

"Spread the word," Jimmy said.

The Chief pushed his chair back from the desk, and Jimmy went around to the front of the desk and plopped down into a chair.

"The only fingerprints found on your desk and chair were yours. Found several paw prints, so your cat's been up there," Chief Price said.

"Yeah, she sits on the desk and watches me type. Sometimes she tries to type, but her paws are too big to hit a specific key," Jimmy said. "I installed motion detectors at the living room windows."

"Good. That will alert that loud bird of yours should anyone attempt a window entry again," the chief said. "So far, we don't have anything else out of Mr. Brown's mouth. Should have some information from the NCIC database today."

"What about that list of the Diaz relatives?" Jimmy asked.

"We're looking at it."

"Can I have a copy? I want to be able to check off anyone I've met," Jimmy said.

"It's only names, no pictures," the chief said.

"Well, if they're all local, I can find pictures online," Jimmy said. "That way, I'll know if I saw them around town, or even back in The Big City."

The chief hit a number on his phone. "Masters, bring in another copy of that list of the Diaz family."

"Sure thing, Chief."

A few minutes later, Celebrity Masters, a vision of an Earthbound goddess with waves of golden hair down her back and amethyst eyes shrouded by long dark lashes, entered the room. After he resumed breathing, Jimmy surmised she was in her early thirties. Her uniform hugged her curves in all the right places, and her wide smile was reflected in those eyes.

"Here you go, Chief," Celebrity said.

"Have you met Katz?" the chief asked.

Celebrity's eyes swung over to Jimmy. "No, I can't say that I have." She extended her hand. "Pleased to meet you."

"The pleasure is all mine," he said as he grasped her hand.

A zing went up his arm and he released her hand.

"Anything in from NCIC?" Chief Price asked.

"Nothing yet. Our internet connection is a bit wonky this morning," Celebrity said. "I'll let you know as soon as we have any more information on Mr. Brown."

Jimmy swallowed as she left the room.

The Chief had a hint of a smile he was trying to hide.

"I don't recall seeing her patrolling. Is she a regular cop, or an office worker?" He knew that sounded lame as soon as the words spilled out of his mouth.

"Masters is a warrior cop," he said, and didn't supply anything else. "Let me get back to this report. I'll let you know if anything else crops up. Be vigilant in your wanderings."

Jimmy left the chief to his hunting and pecking. His eyes scanned the outer room for the blonde beauty, but he didn't see her. He left the police station and drove up Diaz Circle to the big house.

JENKINS LED JIMMY TO THE CONSERVATORY, WHERE they found Betty in a modern-day Annie Oakley outfit, hat included, talking a mile a minute. At first, the reporter thought she was talking to the rather large dieffenbachia tree, but he noticed the earpiece and microphone. He was pretty sure the tree wasn't interested in all that business chatter.

"Dexter, I will give your suggestions some thought. Thank you for calling." Betty pressed her earpiece and ended the call when she spied her great-nephew standing in the doorway. "Hello Jimmy, ready for some action on the gun range?"

"Oh! I didn't know we were going shooting today. Should I change my clothes?" he asked.

"Don't be silly. We'll be out back where my targets are set up," she said. She crossed the floor to a table where two gun cases rested. She handed him one and carried the other. They left the conservatory through French doors to a lovely patio area.

They then walked to an area on the five acres with a large umbrellaed table. Jimmy saw the steel framed shooting targets in the distance. There appeared to be paper targets clipped to the frame.

"Here we go." Betty set her gun case on the table and opened it. "This is my favorite handgun—a Ruger GP100 10mm automatic. I call it my lucky piece."

Jimmy opened his gun case and looked over the handgun. "Yours is a Heckler and Koch VP9 with a 9-round magazine. It should be comfortable to handle," she explained. She showed him the trigger safety, and the firing pin safety, where a red dot appeared when the firing pin was cocked and the gun was ready to shoot.

"Either hold the gun with the barrel up, or down facing the ground, but don't accidentally shoot yourself in the foot," she said. "Keep your finger off the trigger until you're ready to shoot."

Jimmy noticed someone off in the distance to the right of the targets. "Is someone supposed to be out there?"

"That's Toombs. He doesn't want to end up in one, so please don't shoot him. He'll change out the targets for each of us," she said. Betty handed Jimmy some ear plugs. "When you're on the gun range practicing, wear ear protection. You don't want to go deaf at an early age."

They walked to an orange line spray painted on the grass.

The target was seven yards away.

"Let's see how you do at this distance. Toombs can move the target closer if necessary. Stand with your feet shoulder-width apart."

Jimmy followed her directions for the correct posture and how to sight, and how to release the safety.

"Make sure you do not close your eyes. It's imperative to keep your eye on the target at all times," she instructed. "Try to hit the target on the left."

Jimmy aimed for the left target and pulled the trigger. His bullet went through the target two-inches from direct center.

"Well, look at you! That's pretty good for your first time. Try it again."

He sighted and pulled the trigger. This time, he hit the bullseye.

"This time, I want you to keep shooting. Don't stop until you're clicking blanks."

"Ookay! This is fun!"

He let loose a string of bullets until his gun clicked.

She waved to Toombs to bring the target. The man jogged to the target, changed it out with a new paper target, then jogged up to the shooters.

"Mighty fine shooting," Toombs said as he handed Betty the target.

They studied the target.

"Looks like a couple of rounds went through the center." She noted one hole above the center, one wide hole to the right of center. "You're a natural, Jimmy. You just need practice to get very comfortable with your gun. I'll teach you how to dismantle, clean and oil it," Betty said. She stood in position and fired nonstop at the target.

Toombs jogged the target over to them. There was only one large hole through the center.

"I didn't want to intimidate you by going first," Betty said.

"Wow, Aunt Betty, you're a sharpshooter!"

"You will be too, once you're more comfortable with your weapon. Chief Price will verify your skills for a carry license when the time comes," she said. She gave him Toombs' phone number. "Anytime you want to practice, you don't have to wait for me. Call Toombs and he'll set things up."

They practiced for another hour with Toombs changing targets to spinners.

JIMMY ARRIVED HOME, ELATED. HE CARRIED THE gun case upstairs and wondered where he should keep it. He thought the bedside table was too obvious. Same with the dresser, the closet and the desk. In the end, Maddy watched as he slid it under the sofa. He thought that would be the last place someone would expect to find it. Then he stood staring at the sofa and shook his head.

"That's just plain dumb." He retrieved the gun and walked back to his bedroom, and put it in the bedside table.

"He's home!" Guppy announced for all the world to hear.

"What'd you two do while I was gone? Did Mrs. Potts bring you downstairs?"

"Grapes!" Guppy said, none too quietly.

"Did you eat grapes?" Jimmy asked. "Want to go out to the gazebo?

"Freedom!"

Maddy rubbed against his legs. *We love outdoors!*

Jimmy went to the pantry and grabbed the basket and his arm towel. He stood the novel he was reading into the basket and a beer. "All aboard the gazebo express!"

Maddy hopped into the basket, and Guppy climbed onto Jimmy's towel-covered arm. They went downstairs. He stopped at the kitchen, but Mrs. Potts wasn't there. He went outside and walked to the gazebo.

"Okay, let's relax among nature," he said. Guppy settled in his tree, while Maddy walked along the ledge, sat and stared outside.

Jimmy settled on the padded bench and put his feet up. He chugged some beer and listened to the birds chirping and the squirrels scampering through the trees for several minutes. His mind wandered back over the past few months to how his life had changed so completely. There would no longer be episodes of not making ends meet, threats of being evicted, or living in a storage unit.

After a few minutes, he pulled his mind away from that negative thinking. He hadn't broached the subject to ask his aunt why his parents kept her a secret from him. It seemed to be an unmentionable topic, but he decided to bring it up the next time he was at the mansion.

Jimmy pulled the book out of the basket and opened it. He spent the next hour reading, while Maddy raced around the ledge, her tail twitching, watching squirrels, birds and butterflies, and as Guppy squawked at anything that moved.

"Okay, guys. I'm getting hungry. Let's go see what Mrs. Potts is cooking for supper," he said as he stood, replaced the book and the empty beer bottle in the basket and waited for Maddy to hop on board. He held out his arm for his bird, and they left the gazebo.

The house was still quiet, which he thought was odd. Mrs. Potts was always there. He climbed the stairs to his apartment and settled his pets. As he placed the basket in the pantry, his phone rang. He saw that it was his landlady.

"Hi, Mrs. Potts, I was beginning to worry," he said.

"Jimmy, the car broke down and I'm at the garage. I'm afraid the ice cream has melted and the milk may be spoiled. Would you be able to pick me up?"

"Where are you?" he asked.

"Over on Pincher Street at Melvin's Garage. We'll have to make a stop at the Foo."

"Hold tight. I'll be right there." He changed out of his flip-flops and put on sturdier sandals, then headed out the door, calling over his shoulder, "Be back soon. Have to go get Mrs. Potts."

CHAPTER TWELVE

immy pulled up at the garage. Mrs. Potts was flustered. He loaded the bags into the back of the CR-V and drove them to the Foo.

"What happened with your car?" he asked.

"Overheated. Melvin's going to look it over to find the exact problem," she said.

He pulled the car into the Foo parking lot. "Why don't you stay here and take it easy? Tell me what to pick up."

"A gallon of milk, butter pecan ice cream, and—don't tell anyone, but grab something from the freezer for supper. I'm not going to cook tonight," Mrs. Potts said.

"Okay, be right back." He left the keys in the ignition and the AC running so his landlady would stay comfortable.

He entered the store, snagged one of the green plastic hand-held baskets, and darted over to the dairy section. He found the Lactaid whole milk she bought, but they were out of gallons, so he put two half-gallons in the basket. Next, he went to the freezer section and perused frozen entrees. He chose chicken Alfredo, then a package of frozen green beans. As he approached the ice cream section, he recognized the woman approaching him.

"Hi, Celebrity."

"Hi, Jimmy." She scrutinized his basket.

"Just picking up things for Mrs. Potts. Her car broke down and she's outside in my car, frazzled."

"Oh, no. What happened?" Celebrity asked.

"Radiator overheated." He didn't know why he was acting so tongue-tied. The words just would not come out.

"Well, you'd better not keep her waiting," Celebrity said. She gave him a full-out smile, winked and continued on her way.

Wow, he mouthed silently. He almost forgot the ice cream, but came to his senses.

"LET'S GET HOME BEFORE THE ICE CREAM MELTS!" JIMMY belted out, still dazzled by his contact with the lovely Celebrity.

Mrs. Potts' cellphone rang. "Oh, it's Melvin." She clicked to answer the call on speaker. "Hi, Melvin. What's the bottom line?"

"Bertha, I hate to break it to you, but someone sabotaged your hoses," Melvin said.

Mrs. Potts and Jimmy shared a glance with each other, faces covered in a shocked expression.

Jimmy piped up. "Melvin, it's Jimmy Katz. I'm calling Chief Price. Don't do anything else right now. This could be connected to the big problem."

"Oh! Okay. I'll make sure no one goes near the car!"

Jimmy pulled up in front of Mrs. Potts' boarding house and pulled out his own cellphone. "Chief? Mrs. Potts' car was sabotaged. Call Melvin for the details. I told him not to do anything with it."

They heard the Chief belt out orders for someone to get over to Melvin's garage pronto.

"I'm heading over there!" the Chief said.

Jimmy helped carry in the groceries. "Would you be able to feed my animals? I'm going back to the garage."

"Good. I want details and pictures! I'll take care of Guppy and Maddy," Mrs. Potts said.

Jimmy rushed out the door, hopped back into the car, made a quick U-turn, and sped off.

COPS WERE ALL OVER MEL'S GARAGE WHEN JIMMY'S car pulled up and parked out of the way. He walked over to Chief Price.

"Mrs. Potts was at the Foo when it happened," Jimmy said.

"Celebrity, get over to the Foo and check to see if there're any cameras that might have captured anything," Price called out. "Mrs. Potts typically parks up front."

Jimmy and Chief Price walked into the garage and approached Melvin.

"The upper and lower radiator hoses were cut," Melvin said. "Someone used a heavy-duty tool to cut through those two-inch hoses." He pointed out two other hoses that were cut: the heater hoses that supplied hot coolant from the engine to the heater core.

Jimmy took pictures with his phone.

"It's obvious this was deliberate," the Chief said. He nodded to CSI Lloyd to get to work and dust for fingerprints. Since most criminals weren't known for their excessive brain-power to think things through or plan their crime, the Chief felt certain they would find prints. "Let's go over to the Foo."

Jimmy and the Chief drove in separate vehicles. They arrived at the Dime Water Foo(d) store, parked and went inside to hunt down Celebrity. They found her at the customer service booth talking with manager Brink Hellman.

"Any luck with those front cameras?" Chief Price asked.

Hellman waved to follow him back to the stairs leading to the security office. They climbed the stairs and entered the manager's office, along with the security department.

The manager led them into the security area where a slovenly man was shoving a burger into his gaping jaw. Mustard and mayo dripped in front of the keyboard on the desk. The guy rushed to swipe up his mess with a handful of thin napkins, actually just smearing the puddle of condiments around his desk.

He chewed and swallowed, then found his voice. "Sorry, boss. What's going on?"

"Meaty, we've got a problem. Someone deliberately damaged Mrs. Potts' car when she was in the store," Hellman said. "We need you to take a look at the security tapes."

"When did it happen?" Meaty asked.

"Approximately ninety minutes ago," the Chief said.

Meaty wiped his hands with napkins, then rubbed them on his jeans for good measure. One monitor had windows inside a large window showing different views of the store and parking lot.

"Where was she parked, do you know?" Meaty asked.

"She typically parks as close to the front as possible. Want me to call her to get the closest location?" Jimmy asked.

"Nah, she's got that Chevy Equinox, if I remember correctly. Baby blue, right?"

"Yes," Jimmy said. "You should be able to spot the color over any other blue in the parking lot."

Meaty rolled back the camera files. They found Mrs. Potts' vehicle. Everyone watched as Meaty scrolled through the minutes, when suddenly, a suspicious man wearing cargo pants and a T-shirt stopped by her car.

"Grab me a picture of that man!" Chief Price barked out. "Celebrity, do you recognize him?"

"Never saw him before," the stunning blonde said. Meaty captured a close-up of the man's face.

The guy looked over his shoulder, then right and left. He

opened the driver's door and pulled the latch to release the hood. They all watched as he lifted the hood, pulled hefty cutters out of his cargo pants, and cut the hoses. The cutters disappeared back into the cargo pants, the hood was lowered and the man vanished into the parking lot.

"We'll need the entire segment of this event from all the cameras. If you could back up and find when Mrs. Potts arrived, then skip to this vandalism, I'd appreciate it," Chief Price said. He turned to Jimmy. "Going to have to lecture her about keeping her car locked."

Jimmy nodded. "Did you recognize that man?"

The Chief shook his head. "Not sure he's from around here, but then again, I don't know everyone in the county."

"I'll get on it," Celebrity said as she rushed down the stairs.

JIMMY SMELLED DINNER AS HE UNLOCKED THE FRONT door of the boarding house. He heard Guppy in the kitchen. Maddy ran up to him, meowing down the hallway. *Daddy! Daddy! Daddy's home!* She rubbed against his legs until he picked her up and walked with her to the kitchen.

"Hi, Mrs. Potts. The Foo cameras have a picture of the guy in the act," Jimmy said. He set Maddy on the floor, pulled out his phone and showed Mrs. Potts the cut hoses.

"Oh my! How did he cut those big hoses?" she asked.

"The camera caught him pulling these big cutters out of his cargo pants. Didn't take any effort at all," Jimmy said.

Mrs. Potts put her hands on her hips. "Who in the world is behind these acts?"

"I wish I could answer that," Jimmy said. "There's too many coincidences not to connect these things." A thought flew through his head, giving him a tingling feeling, but he pushed it aside, thinking it was too preposterous.

"Well, let's focus on putting food on our plates," Mrs. Potts said. She dished out chicken Alfredo and green beans and set it in front of Jimmy, then served herself. "Tomorrow we'll be back to normal. Dig in."

After finishing, he attempted to help her clean up the kitchen, but Mrs. Potts shooed him upstairs. Jimmy carried Guppy on his arm while Maddy dashed ahead and charged up the stairs. Guppy took up a vigilant position on his fake tree.

"Guard dog time!" the bird hollered.

Jimmy pulled out the desk chair and moved the mouse to wake up the computer as he slid into the chair. Maddy jumped up on the desk and sat down.

"Maddy, bird is spelled with an "i". It's b.i.r.d, not b.r.d." He shook his head. "I swear I'm not cracking up."

The kitten *mreeped* at him, as if thanking him for correcting her spelling faux pax. *Oops! I didn't know.*

"Why don't you type me a message so I can see how you manage," he suggested.

Guppy belted out a squawk. *Don't show Daddy. Animals are not supposed to know how to do that!*

Okay, I won't, Maddy told her friend.

She licked her paw and washed her ear, then hopped down and jumped up on a windowsill.

"Okay, I guess that's your way of telling me it's your secret." While his pets were busy scrutinizing the outdoors, he pulled up the camera files. He watched in silent glee as the kitten grabbed the chewed No. 2 pencil and hit a key. Jimmy covered his face with his hands, shook his head, and stared at the camera file again.

Maddy knocked out *I [heart symbol] Daddy; I [heart symbol] Guppy. I [heart symbol] Pots.*

It took her a long time to write her statements using the pencil to tap the keys. She rested her jaw between statements. She walked around the laptop and stepped on the Return key, then gripped the pencil and finished her handiwork. Each statement was on a separate line.

Jimmy saved the file so it would not be accidentally over-written. He named the MP4 file Maddy Typing-1. He would never scold her or Guppy for watching too much TV ever again. Those children's programs were teaching them how to communicate.

Now, however, it was time for him to look for the Diaz relatives from the list. Diaz was such a common name in the county. He wondered how he could get through the list to find pictures of all of them. After he tried various searches, he settled on the Starlight Diaz family. That pulled up dozens of connected pictures.

He looked over pictures with corresponding names first. Going down the list, he checked off a lot of names but didn't recognize anyone. He studied pictures without names attached. He didn't recognize any of those people either. Discouraged, he closed the browser.

THE NEXT COUPLE OF WEEKS WERE DISASTER-FREE. Jimmy spent mornings with Moses at the Dojo and afternoons with Toombs target practicing.

The police tracked down Dickie Mutulant, the man responsible for vandalizing Mrs. Potts' car. He swore no one put him up to anything. The Chief mocked him with, "So, out of the entire parking lot, you chose this Chevy Equinox instead of the Subaru with paper plates that was beside it?"

"That's what I said," Mutulant said.

Mr. Mutulant was immediately booked and settled into a jail cell, which Chief Price bet he was familiar with.

Jimmy stopped by the Chief's office. "I looked at pictures of ninety percent of the people on that Diaz list. I didn't recognize any, even in passing." He wore an expression of defeat.

"Listen, we're going to get to the bottom of this, don't you worry," Chief Price said, trying to cheer him up.

"This has me thinking about my parents' accident that ended their lives," Jimmy said. "Maybe it wasn't a chance accident."

The Chief sat and mulled that over. "When did that occur?"

"Two years ago." Jimmy let out a huge sigh. "If we find out this is all connected, my great-aunt may need protection."

"Don't you worry about Betty. That place is like Fort Knox, and Betty is like a whirling dervish. She's a black belt not only in Tai Chi but in other modalities. And I'm pretty sure you've seen her shooting during your training sessions. She's a crack shot," the Chief said while trying to ease Jimmy's mind.

"I realize that, but she IS ninety," Jimmy said. "There must be some vulnerabilities we don't know about. She's sharp, and I never would have thought she was that age when I first met her if Bill or Sylvan hadn't mentioned it ahead of time."

"We can step up the patrols on Diaz Circle," the Chief said. "Whoever is behind this may be out of ready cash to hire someone else because we've had some quiet time. In the meantime, I want you to give me all the details about that accident—everything you can remember, no matter how insignificant. I'll call The Big City and have them pull the files and email everything."

When Jimmy left the police station, Chief Price looked up the phone number for a Big City detective who might save him time going through the switchboard and getting put on hold a half dozen times.

"Detective Breeland? This is Kenton Price, chief of police in Twinkle, Texas. We met several years ago at a crime fighters conference."

"Chief Price! Yes, I sure do remember you. How's the town of Twinkle these days? I'll bet it's better than The Big City," Detective Breeland said.

"Well, we've got a situation here that appears to have started in your city. Do you think you can look up a couple of things and send me the files?"

They spoke for several more minutes. Chief Price heard Breeland's keyboard clacking.

"I've got both files. The case from two years ago involving the Katz' fatal accident and the armed robbery of their son a few months ago. Hhmm. I see what you're getting at. May not be a coincidence after all. Let me hunt down some things and I'll get everything to you before day's end."

Chief Price disconnected the call. He pulled out a notepad and listed the events:

1. Evangeline (Eva) Schlumbacher Katz, Jimmy's mother, and Errol Katz, his father, and the fatal car accident in The Big City.

2. Jimmy's armed robbery at the gas station in The Big City.

3. Attempted murder/break-in at Mrs. Potts' boarding house (same suspect as the gas station holdup).

4. Mrs. Potts' automobile vandalism.

Something didn't add up. While it appeared there was no relationship between any of the events, he felt strongly they were connected.

Celebrity chose that moment to enter his office with a piece of paper. "Info on Reuben Brown. He has a rap sheet longer than a gorilla's arm, but no violent crimes. That tells me someone paid him a lot of money to step up his game."

She glanced at his desk. "What're you doing?"

The Chief flipped it around so she could see the list.

"If those first two things are related to the last two things, we've got a mess on our hands," Celebrity said.

"Let's see if Mr. Brown was stupid enough to deposit a big chunk of money in his bank account," the Chief said.

CHAPTER THIRTEEN

Jimmy walked into the DDS office and asked to speak to Stoney. The attorney came out and greeted him, then they walked back to his office.

"I can see something's on your mind," Stoney said.

"I'd like to get more involved in trying to get to the bottom of these problems," Jimmy said. "As a journalist, I think of myself as an amateur private investigator. In the course of our work, we have to dig deep to get all the facts."

"Have you spoken to Chief Price about this? He may not see things the same as you do," Stoney said.

"Stoney, things seem to be escalating," Jimmy said. "Even though we haven't had any situations for the past couple of weeks, I'm positive all these things are connected."

Stoney thought about the happenings, then nodded. "It might be a good idea to enlist your help."

"Thanks. I'll go talk to the Chief," Jimmy said.

JIMMY'S OLD FRIEND BRIAN ARRIVED AT MRS. POTTS' boarding house two days later. He and Jimmy bashed each other's backs in a manly greeting, then did some weird hand signals. Brian moved into the downstairs apartment and got the grand tour of the house.

"It's good to have you here, Brian," Mrs. Potts said.

He shook her hand. "It's good to be here, Mrs. Potts. I like your house."

"Let's go over to Aunt Betty's. I have to stop at the police station first," Jimmy said. They took off in Jimmy's car.

The Chief slid Jimmy's gun carry permit across his desk. "Don't lose this. I had to pull some strings to get it pushed through."

"Thanks."

"Where's your weapon?" the Chief asked. Jimmy hemmed and hawed. "Home."

"Get one of those waist pack things for when you don't wear a jacket. I want you to keep that gun on you at all times when you're in public," the Chief said.

After they finished up at the police station, they went to the big house so Jimmy could introduce Brian to Betty. Jenkins let them in and escorted them to the library, where Betty was scanning the shelves, searching for something.

"Mr. Katz and friend," Jenkins announced.

Betty turned around and scrutinized Brian. "I know you—well, not personally, but aren't you Jimmy's little friend from school?"

Brian and Jimmy exchanged questioning glances.

"How on Earth could you recognize Brian?" Jimmy asked.

"I have your life in pictures," Betty said. That's all she was going to offer up. "Have you had lunch?"

"No, ma'am," Jimmy said.

Betty picked up an extension phone, called the kitchen, and ordered lunch. Over tuna salad sandwiches, chips and cantaloupe chunks in the conservatory, they chatted.

"How long will you be staying in Twinkle, Brian?" Betty asked.

"Probably a few weeks. Jimmy's going to help me figure out what to do with my life," Brian said. "I might research small towns and write a book about city dwellers moving to rural areas."

"You'll figure it out. No one knows what's in your head beside you," Betty said.

THEY DROVE BACK to the boarding house. Brian went to his apartment and Jimmy climbed the stairs. The first thing he did was check the cameras while Maddy was distracted by two birds fighting in the backyard. Guppy hollered out the window as he watched the fracas.

Camera #1 captured Maddy hopping up on his chair, nudging the mouse with her nose, and looking at the screen. He watched as she snagged the yellow pencil in her jaws and tapped a key. It took her a while to type her message. He glanced at the screen and saw one new word on her document: tuna.

He closed the camera file and opened Camera #2. He watched the process from a different angle. After staring at the screen for an overly long time, he closed the file and pulled up his email. There was nothing but a bunch of junk, which he started deleting.

Jimmy discovered an embarrassing email from Gigi that was several weeks old. He deleted it with a shudder and continued to scan and delete three hundred ninety-two emails.

He heard footsteps on the stairs, a tap on his door, and called out. "Door's open."

Brian entered.

"INVADER!" Guppy squawked out.

"Pipe down, Guppy! Don't you remember, Brian?"

Brian walked over to the bird and pulled a handful of sunflower seeds out of his pocket and put them in Guppy's seed cup. "Hi, Guppy! Don't you remember Uncle Brian?"

"Free food!" Guppy said as he snatched up a seed.

Maddy rubbed against Brian's hairy legs.

"Who's this?" Brian asked.

"Meet Maddy. Her mother abandoned her in the backyard. She was just a tiny thing when I found her," Jimmy said.

Brian noticed the motion detectors and the cameras. "Good setup, but they're visible."

"I did the best I could with what I had," Jimmy said.

"Why do you have the..."

"Let's not talk about that right now," Jimmy said, heading Brian off the subject before he said *cameras* out loud. That was a subject he had to think through. He didn't want his best friend to heckle him, but more importantly, he didn't want the animals to know what they were.

"This is a nice setup," Brian said. "I can see why you like it here."

"Other than these attacks, Twinkle is the ideal place to live. No traffic problems, no pollution, no loud music. People are friendly, and the rent is cheap," Jimmy said.

"Like you need cheap rent now," Brian said.

"Well, before I knew about all that, I could make ends meet comfortably with my TIN salary," Jimmy said.

"I can't get over the fact that your great aunt Betty is the matriarch of the entire county. One of these days, we need to find out why your parents hid these details from you," Brian said.

Jimmy shrugged. "I've even called Mr. Wilkinson, our old family attorney. He was shocked to hear that aunt Betty was alive."

"What happened to all your parents' things after they died?" Brian asked.

Jimmy frowned. "I was in a complete fog. I assume that Mr. Wilkinson handled everything."

"You need to call him and ask what happened to your

parents' personal property and paperwork," Brian said. "It would be beneficial for you to go through that paperwork and perhaps uncover some of this mystery."

"I'll call him tomorrow," Jimmy said. "I stayed in our house for the next year, then the house was sold and I moved into an apartment."

"What happened to your furniture?"

Jimmy was embarrassed to admit how low he had gotten. "I hit a couple of bad patches and had to sell it."

"Why the hell didn't you ask me for help?" Brian asked.

"I didn't want to endanger our friendship. Money can cause a lot of problems between friends," Jimmy said. "None of that is important now, but I sure would like some answers."

"Got any beer?" Brian asked.

BETTY HURRIED DOWNSTAIRS, HER WIDE-LEG palazzo pants flapping as she descended. Jenkins carried a tea set headed toward Betty's office. Suddenly, Betty was airborne with a scream that bristled the hair on the back of Jenkins' neck.

"Mrs. Diaz!" The butler dropped the delicate tea set and lurched to the stairs, his arms out wide like a receiver.

Betty flew into him, knocking him backwards onto the floor. She was stunned for a moment. "Jenkins! Jenkins! Are you alright?"

She climbed off the man, pulled her phone out of her pocket and called 9-1-1. "Send an ambulance!"

Within moments, sirens were heard approaching the mansion. The front door flew open and Chief Price's feet thundered across the floor to the grand staircase.

"What happened?" He knelt beside Jenkins and felt for a pulse. "Alive."

Medics rushed into the house and took over.

Someone checked Betty's pulse and determined she was okay. All efforts were focused on the butler.

Chief Price took hold of Betty's elbow and led her away to a chair in a quiet corner. "What happened?"

Betty adjusted her pants back up to her waist, then looked him dead in the eyes. "Something moved on the stairs and I tripped!"

The Chief went up the stairs one-by-one, his eyes staring down. Midway, he discovered a piece of the non-slip rubber stair tread cut out with kitchen twine attached. The twine went through the balustrade to the top of the stairs to the right.

Chief Price grabbed his phone and used the walkie-talkie feature to call his entire police force. "I want this house secured —all entrances and exits! Search the grounds. Ramirez, get in here with your kit; Lloyd's on his way, but it will take him a while!"

He called Jimmy. "Get over to the mansion! Your aunt and Jenkins had an accident."

Detective Ramirez came through the front door. "What do you have?"

The Chief led him over to the stairs. They climbed to the doctored step.

"Amateur, but obviously effective," Ramirez stated. He ran outside and returned with a couple of equipment bags. He pulled a professional camera out of his bag and snapped pictures, then climbed the stairs and found the twine at the top of the staircase. Someone had originally taped it to a floorboard so they wouldn't lose the twine when they were ready to act. He followed the twine to a hiding place, taking pictures along the way.

Half the TIN employees showed up. Sylvan led the stream into the mansion. "What happened?" He saw that Betty was okay. Jenkins was on a gurney being taken outside to an ambulance.

Brian's car screeched to a halt and Jimmy was out the door before the car came to a full stop. His feet thundered into the house with Brian on his heels.

"Aunt Betty! Thank God you're okay! What happened?"

"I was coming down the stairs getting ready to go into a Zoom meeting in my office, when I felt something move under my foot. I went flying! Jenkins blocked my fall!" she said with more than a hint of anger. "There must be a traitor on my staff!"

"Have you hired anyone new?" Jimmy asked.

"Everyone has been here for years," Betty said.

"Somebody must have been paid a lot of money to do this," Sylvan said.

"How many people do you have here?" Jimmy asked the Chief.

"Six."

"Not enough," Jimmy said. He turned to his friend. "I don't know the house that well. I've only been in a couple of rooms downstairs. We're going to have to learn the layout right now. We need to assist the police and go room by room. Search them completely—cabinets, drapes, whatever—anywhere someone could hide. There might be someone who got access to the house without anyone knowing about it." Jimmy turned to the Chief. "Who's rounding up the staff?"

"We haven't gathered them yet," the Chief said with a hint of snippiness. He didn't appreciate someone coming in and taking over his responsibilities, even if it was the heir.

"Listen, I have experience from my journalism career and working with the large police force in The Big City," Jimmy said. "Let's work together and find the culprits behind these things. Attempted murder seems to be rampant in my family."

He focused on Betty. "You round up the staff." He returned his focus to the Chief. "Get your team outside and cover every possible exit/entrance to this house." He turned to the TIN staff. "Can you check all outbuildings, garages and any other structures on the property?"

"You bet," Danny said in a stormy voice. He couldn't believe Jenkins was on the way to the hospital, and Mrs. Diaz had narrowly escaped death.

The TIN staff rushed from the house and gathered outside to divvy up their search.

Chief Price lost his attitude when he recognized that Jimmy had more experience with this type of situation. The Twinkle police department never had a crime spree of this magnitude and it was escalating. They could use all the help they could get. "My team is outside checking all exits".

Brian and Jimmy split up. Brian took the upstairs. Jimmy trolled the downstairs. Betty called all the staff members to the kitchen.

Jimmy figured he'd start in the kitchen and work his way outward through the downstairs rooms. He checked the butler's pantry, which contained the cleaning supplies cabinet and the broom, vacuum, mops and pails cabinet. Then he checked every cabinet in the kitchen, including the cabinets under the island.

Next up was the dining room. No cabinets, but he checked the long sidebar with doors underneath. He moved to the library. No cabinets, only shelves. The conservatory. No cabinets, only plants, pillars, and wispy drapes no one could hide behind. He checked the small reading room, the living room, Betty's office, which contained a large supply cabinet.

Betty's bedroom, bathroom, and closets were large enough

to hide an entire gang, but no one was flattened against walls or floors, or in deep shadows. He moved on to the last room, the gym, and the connected bathroom/shower. No place to hide in the actual gym, and the bathroom contained a singular shower stall, toilet and sink. Towels were stored on open shelves. No place to hide. Jimmy headed back to the kitchen.

Upstairs, Brian checked the room where the twine had ended. Ramirez was shining his light and dusting for fingerprints instead of waiting for CSI Lloyd to show up. Brian went through all the bedrooms, bathrooms, the common lounge area, linen closets and any other space that had a door or cabinets. There were plenty of thick drapes where someone could hide, but not even dust bunnies lurked anywhere.

Brian returned to the first floor and wandered back to the kitchen, where he found Betty with her staff.

"Everyone accounted for?" Jimmy asked her as he entered the room.

Betty wore a grim expression. "Josie is missing. She hasn't answered my calls or texts."

The other staff members were seated at the kitchen table. They murmured among themselves, shocked over their missing coworker, the botched death trap that almost killed their boss, and their friend, Jenkins.

Chief Price entered the kitchen. Jimmy brought him up to date regarding Josie. The Chief pulled his phone out. "Stephanie, put an APB out on Josie Rigton." He turned to Betty and the staff. "What does she drive?"

"A Toyota 4Runner," one employee said. "1996, black with a lot of bondo, and no rear bumper."

The Chief fed the information into the phone as Celebrity walked into the kitchen.

"Get banking information on this woman," the Chief instructed. "Let's see if she made a large deposit recently."

Betty plopped into a chair. "I can't believe one of my own staff would do this."

Her employees tried to comfort their beloved employer and matriarch of the community.

The TIN group wandered into the kitchen, led by Sylvan. "We checked all six garage slots, and any conceivable hiding place, even up in the attic."

Bill swatted a cobweb from his head. "There's no standing room over the garage."

"We checked the toolshed, the potting shed, and a couple of the small spaces with Toombs," Danny said. "Do you think someone could be hiding in the bushes? There's five acres, after all."

"Anyone see a 4Runner leaving the property?" the Chief asked.

The TIN staff all shook their heads.

"Betty, let's get over to the hospital and check on Jenkins. He may have seen something," the Chief said.

"I'm coming with you," Jimmy said. He turned to Brian. "I'll meet you back at the house."

CHAPTER FOURTEEN

Jenkins had a serious concussion, Dr. Canada informed them. The doctor's name was pronounced Kah Nod Ah, instead of the pronunciation for the country north of the USA.

"He's going to have to stay put for a couple of days. I want to make sure he doesn't have any complications," Dr. Canada said. "He had quite a fall, and I'm surprised he didn't split his skull open. We performed a CT scan, and I'll order an MRI tomorrow."

Betty fussed over the butler in the hospital bed.

"Can I question him?" the Chief asked.

"Keep it simple, and don't get him riled up," Dr. Canada said.

The Chief moved to the bedside. "Jenkins, did you see anyone upstairs when Mrs. Diaz tripped?"

Jenkins looked a little green from nausea. "Not sure."

Chief Price decided it would be better to wait until the next day for further questioning. Jenkins was currently too sick and unable to focus due to the concussion.

He tapped Betty on the shoulder. "We should let him rest."

She nodded. The Chief and Jimmy escorted her out of the hospital room.

PLOT TO KILL BETTY KATZ-DIAZ THWARTED BY BUTLER

THE TIN HEADLINES had the phones ringing at the

newspaper office and the police station nonstop. The Biggem Diner and other eating places were filled with people buzzing over cups of coffee. People shared information with neighbors over fences. No matter where you looked in Twinkle, or across the county, heads were together and lips were flapping the news and their opinions.

The small article under the headline listed some facts, but didn't provide the exact details of the incident.

Last night at six pm., Mrs. Betty Diaz, widow of Clem's Corner founder Clemento Diaz, and the Katz-Diaz matriarch, was saved from what the police said could have been a fatal fall down the main staircase, by her loyal butler of 22 years, J.B. Jenkins.

Jenkins caught Mrs. Diaz as she tripped on a deliberate obstruction on one of the stairs.

Jenkins is recovering from injuries at the Starlight General Hospital under the care of Dr. Irving Canada. Discharge from the hospital will be considered after evaluation of pending medical test results. "Mrs. Betty," as she is fondly known, was not injured.

Josie Rigton, an employee of ten years at the Diaz mansion, was at large and wanted for questioning. Police request that anyone with information regarding Rigton contact them immediately.

JIMMY WALKED into the TIN office via the rear parking lot door. Both Bill and Sylvan were sitting in the newsroom with their feet up on open desk drawers.

"Anyone get any sleep last night?" Jimmy asked.

"Man, since you've come to town, we've had more news than we know what to do with," Danny said.

Jimmy pulled out the chair at his desk and pondered for a minute. "It started before I came to town."

Both Bill and Sylvan sat upright with shocked expressions on their faces, their feet hitting the floor.

"What are you saying?" Sylvan asked.

"Chief Price is looking into it, but it started when I was held up at the gas station in The Big City, and may go back to the automobile accident that killed my parents," Jimmy said.

Everyone stared at him in disbelief.

"You can't print that yet. All you can do is make a file. Hopefully, we'll discover who's behind this soon. We're pretty sure we know why—the Katz-Diaz fortune," Jimmy said.

Danny pulled out a small tape recorder. "I want the details. We won't print anything until the finish line, and you, Betty, and the Chief approve, but I want to see the whole picture."

Jimmy spent the next ninety minutes laying out the details of everything that had happened. "I promise to let you know if anything else sheds light on these events. I just want whoever is behind this brought to justice. I pray that my parents weren't murdered."

"Any word on the APB for that housemaid?" Sylvan asked.

Jimmy shook his head. "Haven't heard anything from the Chief yet."

"How's Jenkins?" Bill asked.

"I'm going to pick up Aunt Betty and we're going over to the hospital," Jimmy said. "Dr. Canada should have the MRI results by then."

"Thank God he was there to save Betty," Sylvan said. "Are you carrying?"

Jimmy pulled the left side of his jacket aside to show his shoulder holster and the Heckler and Koch VP9. "The Chief put a rush on the carry permit."

"Make sure you park in the open and don't walk in any shadows," Bill said.

"I wish I had my mother's eyes that were in the back of her head—she always seemed to see everything I was doing, even when I thought I was hiding things," Jimmy said.

"Yeah, mothers seem to have that sixth sense when it comes to kids," Sylvan said. "And even kids who were friends of their kids."

"Take care, man," Danny said.

JIMMY LEFT THROUGH THE BACK DOOR AND GOT INTO HIS car. He steered out of the parking lot, turned left on Jiltson Way, right on Stonerich, then onto Diaz Circle. He pulled into the parking area of the mansion, clicked the fob and locked the car doors, something he was not used to doing since moving to Twinkle.

The heir pressed the doorbell and heard the gong. He was surprised to see Toombs in butler's clothes answering the door.

"Hi, Toombs. Is my Aunt Betty ready?" Jimmy asked.

"Come in, Mr. Jimmy, she's in her office," Toombs said.

Jimmy went directly to his great-aunt's office. "Hi, Aunt Betty. Is everything okay?"

"I've been thinking about all this, Jimmy, and I told the Chief that two years ago, just before your parents were killed in that accident, I made changes to my will," Betty said. "I have a whole list of bequeaths to people. I'm the only one, aside from DDS, who knew of your existence. If anything happened to me, they would have found you and brought you to Twinkle, but as luck had it, you just showed up."

"Had you cut anyone out of your will?" Jimmy asked.

"No, but I had adjusted some of the bequeaths, and special

endowments," she said. "Someone must have accessed my files. That's all I can think of."

"Do you keep your computer locked?" he asked.

"I just changed the password. If anything happens to me, you can access my computer using my maiden name: Katz, which on the phone would be 5289. My folders are very organized, and they are backed up to the cloud and an external hard drive that I keep in the safe," Betty said.

"Do the attorneys have the safe combination and an inventory of what's in there?" Jimmy asked.

"Yes. I've instructed them to pass the combination over to you upon my demise," she said. "Hopefully, that won't be anytime soon. There's so much I need to share with you about the Katz and the Diaz families."

"You're my only living relative, Aunt Betty," Jimmy said, somewhat forlorn.

"Cheer up, sonny boy. I'm not dead yet, and it will take more than flying down the stairs to stop me. Poor Jenkins!"

"We'd better get going. I'm not sure how long visiting hours are," Jimmy said.

"When you build the hospital, the rules no longer apply," Betty said with a wink.

Jimmy smiled as he escorted her out of the house.

JENKINS HAD THE HEAD OF THE BED ELEVATED SO HE could sit up. He no longer looked green and perked up when he saw Aunt Betty walk through the door, followed by Jimmy.

Betty rushed over to the hospital bed with the exuberance of a mother checking on one of her chicks.

"Jenkins! How are you today? Are you still experiencing nausea or headaches?" Betty inquired.

"I'm better, and I hope the doctor will release me so I can go home." Home was the mansion where he had lived for the past twenty-two years since he was twenty-one right out of butler school.

Betty turned to Jimmy. "Can you hunt down Dr. Canada and find out about Jenkins' release? We need to be here to fetch him home."

"Sure," Jimmy said. He left the room and headed to the nurses' station.

"Jenkins, so much has happened. You're not going to believe what I have to report. I'm saddened to say that Josie seems to be the one behind the incident on the stairs. She's missing," Betty said.

"Josie?" Jenkins gasped. "No! I can't believe anyone on staff would ever harm you!"

"Hon, when someone dumps a boat-load of money in your lap, things flip in your head," Betty said. "It's all in the hands of the police now."

Chief Price waltzed into the room. "What's in our hands now? I think we have enough going on." He walked up to the bed and looked Jenkins over. "You look a heck of a lot better today. Can you remember seeing anything yesterday at the time of the accident?"

Jenkins shook his head. "I've had the entire scenario run through my head over and over, and I don't recall seeing anyone upstairs on the landing."

"She won't get far. I've got an APB out statewide. Damn shame she didn't come forward to tell someone about this treachery prior to deciding to participate," Chief Price said. He turned to Betty. "There was a twenty thousand dollar deposit in her checking account, but then she must have thought better about it, or the person who hired her warned her about the consequences.

She closed the account so we can't track her by debit card expenses."

"Twenty thousand dollars? Is that all I'm worth to her? I can't believe she gave up her position for that paltry sum!" Betty bemoaned.

"Betty, something must have happened in the near past to make her want to harm you. Was she ever rebuked for something? Did she have a bad annual review?" the Chief asked.

A thought flashed through Jenkins' eyes. "You elevated Elnora to your personal helper. Maybe Josie thought that should have been her new post?"

Betty was quiet for a moment. "Elnora is much more refined and put-together, and I knew she would be perfect for the position. Josie was housemaid material, hands down. Oh, lord, could that have been the turning point for her?"

"Well, at least now we know that was bottled up inside her. She must have said something to a compassionate listener—our unknown suspect," Chief Price said.

Jimmy returned with Dr. Canada.

"You ready to get out of here, Jenkins?" Dr. Canada asked his patient. "The scans didn't turn up any brain bleeding or anything else that would keep you here."

"When will he be released?" Betty asked. "Can we take him home with us now?"

Dr. Canada nodded. "I don't see any reason to keep him here. Just make sure he takes it easy for the rest of the week. He's one stubborn man."

THEY DROVE Jenkins home and Betty got him situated in his room. She then brought Jimmy up to date about Josie.

"Twenty grand isn't a lot of money," he said. "Do you think she's headed to Mexico?"

"I can't see her wanting to escape to the south. I'd guess Canada," Betty said.

"Have the police searched her place? Maybe they could find correspondence with whoever paid her," Jimmy said. He turned thoughtful. "Aunt Betty, when my parents died, were you the one who paid for everything, or was it all through the life insurance policy? I don't know what happened to my parents' possessions and private papers."

Betty looked questioningly at Jimmy. "No, the insurance company must have paid for everything. You should have inherited the house and contents. You didn't?"

Jimmy shook his head. "No, I didn't receive any insurance money or anything."

"Have you spoken to the attorney? He should have all the details. I don't understand why everything was sold. You were their only child," Betty said. "Something is not adding up, Jimmy. I think you should sit down with Chief Price and go over all of this."

"I was going to call the attorney today to find out what happened to my parents' important papers," Jimmy said. "Maybe I should hold off until I speak to the Chief."

"That sounds like a better plan. Get with the Chief," Betty said.

Jimmy took off and went to the police station. "Is the big man available?" he asked Sgt. Gonzales.

"Getting bigger by the second!"

Jimmy walked back to the Chief's office where Celebrity, Ramirez, and Chief Price were looking through paperwork. "Knock, knock."

The Chief looked up. "Jimmy! Glad you're here. I've got a list of questions for you."

Celebrity got up and brought another chair she stole from the outer room. "Here, sit."

"This Wilkinson is the family attorney in The Big City?" the Chief asked.

"Yes," Jimmy said. "Aunt Betty and I were just talking about him. Something's not right."

"That's the bottom line. Brian mentioned you didn't know what happened to your parents' personal papers. Is that right?" Chief Price asked.

"Yes, that and how the estate was handled. Aunt Betty said she didn't have anything to do with paying all the expenses, selling our house, and everything else. Plus, I never received any life insurance, which she said was odd," Jimmy said.

"Do not contact the attorney, and don't talk to any outsiders about any of this," the Chief said.

"Do you think he's behind this?"

"He's one of the players," Celebrity said. "But he's not working alone."

Jimmy was shellshocked. Just then, his cellphone dinged an incoming text. At first, he wasn't sure what to make of it because it said it was from Home. He clicked on it and read one word: HELP.

"Something's happening at home!"

They were all instantly out of their seats and out the door.

Cars barreled down Stoneridge Boulevard led by the Chief's car, siren screaming and lights flashing. They raced around the corner to Burbridge St., with Celebrity making a wide turn and coming to a haphazard stop on the lawn, her tires spitting up dirt and grass. The Chief slammed on his brakes before crashing into the porch. They were all out of their cars within seconds with Jimmy in the lead to unlock the front door.

They heard Guppy screeching out *INVADERS* through the open upstairs living room windows.

Jimmy raced up the stairs with feet thundering after him. He slammed open his apartment door, gun drawn. A stranger had his two hands on Guppy, getting ready to wring his neck.

Jimmy charged into the room, gun arm outstretched, both hands on his weapon, and an ugly expression on his face. "Remove your hands off my bird's neck before I put a bullet right through your ear!" He didn't see Maddy anywhere, and the place was a wreck. He cocked his gun.

The man, in a grimy T-shirt and oil-stained jeans, carefully pulled his hands away from Guppy. "Don't shoot!" He raised his hands in the air.

Guppy fluffed his feathers, stretched his neck and bit the man's chin.

"OW!" the guy hollered.

The Chief barreled into the room, followed by Celebrity and Ramirez. He placed one hand on Jimmy's arm that was holding the gun and forced his arm down. "We'll take it from here. Don't do anything foolish."

Celebrity dashed around them, cuffed the intruder and read him his rights.

The bookcase was knocked over. Papers were all over the floor, furniture knifed open with stuffing sticking out.

"Maddy!" Jimmy raced around the apartment, searching for the kitten. He finally found her in the pantry, hiding behind a tall container of oatmeal. Jimmy scooped her up. "Oh, Maddy! You gave me a fright when I couldn't find you. Did you send daddy a text? What a smart little girl!"

She reached up and pressed a paw against his lips. *A bad man was going to hurt Guppy!*

CHAPTER FIFTEEN

"Where's Mrs. Potts and Brian?" The Chief asked.

"I don't know," Jimmy said as he walked into the living room carrying Maddy. "Probably grocery shopping."

The downstairs door opened. "Jimmy? What's happened?" Danny Stonerich hollered. He and his father rushed up the stairs. A moment later they all heard a car door slam shut.

"Jimmy! Guppy! Maddy!" Mrs. Potts yelled with fright. She barreled up the front stairs, onto the porch and into the house.

"Jimmy—what the hell?" Brian hollered.

Celebrity hauled the perpetrator down the stairs past Mrs. Potts and Brian, and out the front door, handcuffed. Everyone else tramped downstairs. Jimmy calmed his landlady.

"Some guy got in and tore my place apart," Jimmy said. "Guppy was hollering, and he was going to wring Gup's neck."

"Oh, NO!" Mrs. Potts almost swooned. "And Maddy? Is she okay?"

"Yes. They're both okay. I have no idea who that guy is or what he was looking for," Jimmy said.

"Let's sit down," the Chief said.

"I'll make coffee after I bring the grocery bags inside," Mrs. Potts said.

"I'll get them," Brian said. He went outside, then returned with two of her reusable sacks.

They all went to the kitchen. The Chief, Jimmy, and Brian sat at the table, while Mrs. Potts brewed a pot of breakfast blend coffee. Danny and Sylvan leaned against the counter.

"I spoke with Detective Breeland, a Big City detective, I had the pleasure of meeting at a conference a few years back," Chief Price said. "He pulled the case files from your parents' accident, and your holdup at the gas station."

Everyone prepared their coffee.

"There seemed to be something strange surrounding that accident because it wasn't investigated thoroughly. I read a statement by your attorney that said he recalled your father was having problems with the car prior to the accident," the Chief said.

Both Jimmy and Brian balked.

"My father maintained his vehicles himself. Brakes, hoses, oil changes," Jimmy stated. "He even rebuilt a transmission once. And he never would have driven any vehicle that was having mechanical problems."

"Well, we can't examine the car now. It was most likely scrapped," the Chief said. "But we can pick apart the contents of the file."

"What about the holdup?" Jimmy asked. "I can't see how that was planned unless someone had been following me."

"A stolen car pulled into the gas station behind you," the Chief said. "I watched the camera feed, and it was not a random holdup. The perpetrators abandoned the stolen car and beelined to yours."

Jimmy and Mrs. Potts were dumbstruck.

"This MUST be coming from The Big City," Mrs. Potts stated. "No one in Twinkle would ever think to do these terrible things!"

"Unfortunately, I think you're wrong," the Chief said. "There IS someone in Twinkle who is orchestrating these events. We just don't know who. The goons we have taking up jail space haven't given up their boss yet, and it's getting crowded in there. Hopefully, when we get Josie into custody, she'll open things up for us."

"Jimmy, have you made a list of everyone you've met in Twinkle?" Sylvan asked.

"No, but that's pretty easy," he said. He started with the TIN office. Then the people he interviewed for articles. Mrs. Potts' nephews. Divinia Reynolds. The DDS attorneys. The Diaz household employees. Doc Halliday. Hector and Jorge. Annie and Horace at the Bull Ride. "I can't really think of anyone else."

"Let's face it," Danny said. "He's been all over the place, including various stores, bars and restaurants."

The doorbell rang. Mrs. Potts went to the door. She greeted Divinia Reynolds, the librarian.

"Bertha! Are you okay? I was appalled to see police cars on your lawn. Celebrity and I passed each other just now, and it looked like someone was in the back seat of the police car," Divinia said.

Jimmy joined his landlady at the door.

"There's been an unfortunate incident, but everything's okay," Mrs. Potts said. She patted Jimmy's arm.

Jimmy caught a slight downward curl of the librarian's mouth and a frown that quickly changed to a shocked face. "Tore up my place searching for something."

"You're not going back to The Big City, are you?" Divinia asked. "There's been so many things happening to you here in such a short time."

"Heck no!" Jimmy said. "I would never consider living in The Big City again. I love the country's hometown atmosphere with friendly people and a much slower pace."

"I'm so happy to hear that," the librarian said. "We'd hate to lose you!" She turned to Mrs. Potts. "Is there anything I can do for you?"

"Thanks, Divinia, but everything is okay, and the Chief is working the case."

"Well, I'll be on my way then," Divinia said.

Jimmy and Mrs. Potts watched as she walked to her car and drove off.

"Odd. I wonder why she isn't at the library?" Jimmy said. They returned to the kitchen.

Danny rinsed his cup, then his father's cup, and placed them in the sink. "We're gonna head out."

"We won't print another headline, just a short statement on page three," Sylvan said.

The Chief nodded. "Kind of difficult to hide things in a small town, but people have a right to know what's going on."

After the Stonerichs' left, the Chief eyeballed Jimmy. "How did you know there was someone here? Did a neighbor tip you off?"

Jimmy bit his lower lip while contemplating how to break the news. "I received a text." He held out his phone, and they saw the one word: HELP.

"Who sent that? There was no one here. You were at my office, and Mrs. Potts and Brian were at the store."

Jimmy's eyes darted from the Chief to his landlady, then to his best friend. "You're not going to believe it, but Maddy sent the text."

"Maddy? Your cat?" the Chief asked, staring at him hard.

Jimmy nodded. "She's learned how to communicate."

"Must be all those children's shows she watches!" Mrs. Potts said.

"Jimmy, come on!" Brian said.

"Look, I can prove it," Jimmy said as he stood.

The Chief, Mrs. Potts and Brian followed him upstairs. "Remember when that *cat* and *brd* showed up on my laptop? I suspected, but wanted to prove what was going on. That's why

I ordered two cameras along with the motion detectors," Jimmy said as he stood in front of the desk. He righted the lamp, retrieved the laptop from the floor and grabbed the chair.

"Will your laptop still work?" Mrs. Potts asked.

"Yeah, they're sturdy," Brian said.

Jimmy woke his laptop then pulled up the camera files. They watched the intruder as he tore things apart. Then they saw Maddy hop onto the desk chair, grab the pencil in her jaws, whack the blue Message icon, tap the caps lock key, and tap out each letter of one word: H E L P. As soon as she sent the message she jumped down and ran to the pantry and hid behind the big oatmeal container.

They all looked around to discover Maddy batting the sofa stuffing across the floor.

"I can't believe what I just saw!" Chief Price said.

"You can't tell anyone!" Jimmy said. "No one can ever tell anyone about this. If word got out, the government would confiscate her and do God knows what type of experiments— probably open up her head to look into her brain!"

"We have to make a pact," Mrs. Potts whispered. She held her hand out. Jimmy placed his hand on top of hers. Next, Brian placed his hand on top of Jimmy's and the Chief's hand came down on top of the stack.

"The four of us will only speak of these things among ourselves," the Chief said.

"No one can ever discuss this in public," Brian said.

"It is our duty to protect this little kitten! Guppy, too," Mrs. Potts said.

"Thank you for being my friends," Jimmy said.

The front door opened. They heard footsteps heading toward the kitchen.

"Chief?" Celebrity called out.

"Up here," the Chief hollered.

Celebrity climbed the stairs. "Dumped our guy in a cell."

JIMMY, Brian and Celebrity stopped off at the Bull Ride. Mrs. Potts was all tuckered out from the events of the afternoon, and the Chief had to attend to the newest guy that now sat in a jail cell. They piled into chairs at a table and ordered beers.

"We have got to be overlooking something," Celebrity said.

"Well, if you figure it out, let me know," Jimmy said. "This is getting old."

Brian lowered his voice. "I can't get Mr. Wilkinson out of my head. He's been your family attorney... forever!"

"He's the worst traitor ever," Jimmy said. "I wonder when he started thinking and planning... before or after my parents died?"

"As the attorney for the estate, he most likely arranged for everything to go through his office instead of going to you, direct, Jimmy," Celebrity said. "That's the only way all the funeral expenses were taken care of. It's surprising to hear your parents had a full funeral with nice caskets. It would seem that someone who is embezzling from the estate wouldn't want to part with the money."

"Perhaps he wasn't pulled into this business until after the funeral," Brian said.

"That makes sense because that seems to be when I was no longer in the loop. Unfortunately, my head wasn't in the right place to question anything that happened after the funeral," Jimmy said. "I never stopped to think about what happened to the money from the house sale, or where my parents' posses-sions disappeared to."

"Someone obviously took advantage of your lowest point. In fact, I'd bet they most likely counted on it to pave the way for a clear embezzlement," Celebrity said.

Jimmy slugged down his beer and shook his head. "I so want to beat the crap out of Mr. Wilkinson."

"We'll each hold one of his arms while you work him over," Brian said.

THE NEXT MORNING AFTER HIS WORKOUT WITH Moses, Jimmy headed over to the mansion for his session with Toombs. He tromped through the acreage to the gun range.

They shook hands.

"Everything okay over here?" Jimmy asked.

"Jenkins is up and about, but Mrs. Diaz is keeping tabs on him so he doesn't overdo it," Toombs said.

"He could have split his head open on that floor," Jimmy said.

They stood side-by-side and whammied the targets with their chosen handguns. By the time they emptied the maga-zines, smoke hung in the air.

"You're a natural," Toombs said as they walked to the targets. "Make sure you have a full magazine in your weapon at all times and carry a spare magazine on your person."

Jimmy shook his head. "I don't want to be some walking gunfighter, Toombs. What if I pull my gun on the wrong person? What happens if I accidentally shoot someone?"

"It depends on the circumstances, Jimmy. It's better to apol-ogize than to die," Toombs said.

They walked to the house and went through the mudroom

door. Jimmy searched for his great-aunt and found her in the conservatory, staring into space.

"Hi, Aunt Betty. You okay?"

"Hi, Jimmy. I'm just thinking about all the trauma and drama that's happened over the past few weeks. Country living has become dangerous," she said.

"Aunt Betty, don't say that. These are unique circumstances. Someone out there has become greedy. We've worked out that Mr. Wilkinson has embezzled from my parents' estate, but that didn't start until after their funeral," Jimmy said. "Whoever caused that automobile accident coached Mr. Wilkinson through the police investigation to make it appear like a car malfunction associated with regular wear and tear."

"I can't imagine who would plot such a thing. I wonder how much money they got?" Betty said.

"The Chief is most likely working on that," Jimmy said.

Jenkins entered the room with the mail.

"Are you okay?" Jimmy asked the butler.

"I've got a hard head, not to worry," Jenkins said with a little smile.

"So, no one has heard from Josie?" Jimmy asked.

Betty shook her head. "It seems strange to me. I don't know how she could have slipped out of sight and avoided an APB. She wasn't very good at planning her workday, so I have a hard time thinking she was capable of pulling off the tripping episode, then disappearing so successfully."

Her great-nephew stood. "I'm going to drop in and see Chief Price." He bent and kissed her on the cheek. "Everyone should be on alert. If one of your staff could be bought, maybe someone else could."

JIMMY ENTERED THE POLICE STATION AND WAS spotted by Celebrity as soon as the door closed behind him. She headed his way.

"You okay?" she asked. "Looks like you're focused on something."

"Need to see where the Chief is with things. Do you know if he's determined how much was embezzled from my parents' estate?"

"He's been huddled with Ramirez for a while. Let's go see what they've come up with," Celebrity said.

They walked over to the Chief's office. Celebrity didn't announce herself or knock on the door. She barreled inside, one of the perks of a small-town police department—everyone thought they were privy to the Chief in their own special way.

"Hey, Chief, company!" she announced.

The Chief and Ramirez looked up from their paperwork. "Come on in and sit down," the Chief said. "Detective Breeland included a copy of your parents' will in his paperwork. This makes us feel certain that the attorney didn't become involved until after your parents were buried, otherwise the will would not have been included."

"Have you determined how much was embezzled?" Jimmy asked.

"We found the insurance policy," Ramirez said. "You would have received over two-million dollars because of the accidental death clause. The house sold for more than a half-million, and it looks like there was an estate sale for the furnishings."

Jimmy stared through Ramirez in disbelief. He thought back to the time when he and Guppy lived in the storage unit. He was furious. The thought that kept popping into his head was *why was someone doing this to him?* He couldn't dismiss it.

"None of those guys are talking?" he asked.

"Their lips are shut tight," the Chief said.

"Have any of them had visitors? Wives or girlfriends?" Jimmy asked.

"A woman came yesterday to see Robert Fayette," Celebrity said.

"Maybe we can get to him through her and make him divulge who hired him," Ramirez said.

CHAPTER SIXTEEN

The Chief clacked on his computer keyboard and brought up the visitation log. He went into the log and noted a woman with a local phone number as the visitor. "Janet Carrolmath. Doesn't indicate whether she's the wife, girlfriend, sister or friend. Only that she was here during visiting hours and stayed for forty-five minutes."

"Want me to go talk to her?" Celebrity asked.

"Take Ramirez with you. He can scare people senseless just looking at them," Chief Price said with a quirk of his lips. He looked at the digital record and called out an address in Pancake.

Detective Ramirez was out of the chair and on his feet. Celebrity followed him out the door. They flipped a coin in the parking lot to see who would get behind the wheel. Ramirez won.

They drove through the county to Pancake, Texas, a farming community of eight-hundred. The address they needed was in what was referred to as Little Pancake by the locals, a polite way of saying the slums. Mobile homes in various states of crumbling.

Vehicles on cinder blocks. Front yards cluttered with old appliances and whatnot in between knee-high weeds and grass. Kids running around half-naked. Dogs barking. Cats sunning stretched out on junk heaps.

"I hate coming over here," Celebrity said. "My grandfather said Pancake used to be a rich farming community until right after World War II, then for some reason, and he didn't know why, Little Pancake sort of mushroomed up overnight."

"Happens," Ramirez said. "People lose their jobs, turn to the bottle or drugs, and gather where other disenfranchised people have cobbled communities together."

"There has to be a better way of helping people," Celebrity said.

"Cel, some people don't want to be helped," Ramirez said.

"How can you say that? Deep down, everyone wants a better life," she stated.

Ramirez slowed the car. "2245?" He nodded at the deplorable trailer with the screen door hanging by one hinge and boards across cinder blocks for stairs to the front door that hadn't seen paint in over a decade.

He pulled the car over to the side of the road, as there was no evidence of a driveway. They got out, and he hit the key fob and locked the car up tight.

They walked through the knee-high weeds to the door. Ramirez took the front position. He climbed the rickety stairs and rapped on the door. The door was yanked open by a belligerent elderly man in stained briefs with a bulging belly and a raggedy tank-top. He swayed in the doorway, gripping a shotgun aimed at the detective.

Celebrity instantly drew her gun. "Put the shotgun down!"

Ramirez didn't move a muscle. He could smell the booze reeking from the guy's pores, along with a strong whiff of smoked pot.

"Daddy! What are you doing?" a woman called out, panicky.

"You git in your room, Janet! Don't come out 'lessen I call you," the man identified as *Daddy* growled out.

"Put the gun down before they shoot you! Give it here!" the voice known as Janet said.

A hand came out of the shadows, palm up, fingers wiggling, waiting for the man to deposit the weapon in it. After somewhat of a Mexican standoff, the old drunk lowered the shotgun. The hand snatched the weapon before *Daddy* could change his mind. *Daddy* stumbled into the shadows.

Ramirez remembered to breathe again.

After a long moment, Janet came to the doorway. She was a haggard woman who looked fifty, but was more than likely no older than thirty-five and beaten down by the ramifications of her life.

Celebrity was still in a defensive mode with her handgun pointed at the door. "Has the shotgun been secured?"

"Yes, ma'am! Please don't arrest Mr. Fayette. He's dying of cirrhosis of the liver and doesn't know what he's doing half the time," Janet said. "He's in the back now, probably passed out."

Celebrity relaxed her stance, waited for a long moment, then holstered her pistol.

"Are you Janet Carrolmath?" Ramirez asked.

"Yes, I am," she said. "Why would the police be here looking to talk to me?"

"Ms. Carrolmath, you visited Robert Fayette at the jail yesterday," Ramirez said. "We'd like to ask you some questions."

Celebrity approached the stairs. She slid up by Ramirez and surreptitiously tugged his jacket hem. She wanted to take over the line of questioning before the woman shut down from his brusque manner.

"Janet—is it okay if I call you Janet?" Celebrity asked.

"Sure," Janet said, her eyes leaving Ramirez and swerving over to Celebrity. "What's this all about?"

"Well, there seems to be someone who got Robert into trouble," Celebrity said. "We've got two other guys who have been listening to the same person getting them into trouble, and the jail is filling up. We're trying to find out who this mysterious person is so we can put a stop to these offenses."

"I'm not sure I understand you," Janet said.

"Someone hired your Robert to do something bad. We caught him, but he won't tell us who sent him to do this job. Do you know if he was paid ahead of time for this job?" Celebrity asked.

Janet's hand went to a silver chain around her neck. She shook her head. "Bobby hasn't told me anything. I didn't even know what he was picked up for."

"Would you be able to visit him again and ask him some questions for us?" Celebrity asked.

"You want me to wear a wire and spy for you?" Janet balked, somewhat confrontationally.

Ramirez, seeing how the interview was heading, jumped in. "Look, Janet, Bobby isn't in big trouble right now. At most, he's looking at a misdemeanor and a couple of months' of jail-time or community service. If he helps us out, that time could be commuted."

Janet stared at Ramirez, weighing her options. "If he asks me if I'm wearing a wire, I'm not going to lie to him."

"I want you to think about something for a minute," Ramirez said. "If Bobby wasn't paid for this job ahead of time, he's not going to see any money. If he was paid, you need to find out how much and what he did with the money."

Ramirez and Celebrity could see Janet working that out in her head. She could really use some money right about now. If Bobby had money hidden, she wanted it.

"Okay. I'll do it," Janet said. "But I'm not getting into a cop car. When do you want to do this? Can you wait until tomorrow? Schools almost out and my boys will be home soon."

"Tomorrow's fine," Celebrity said. "Can you be at the Twinkle police station by nine o'clock in the morning?"

Janet nodded.

"Okay." Celebrity pulled a card out of her pocket and

handed it to Janet. "If you need a ride at the last minute, give me a call. I'll pick you up in a regular car."

Janet took the card. She read the front of the card and turned it over, but the back was blank, white. "Okay." She stood back and closed the door.

Celebrity and Ramirez returned to the car and took off. "I hope she doesn't back out," Celebrity said.

"We can't force her to cooperate, but just by planting the idea that there was money somewhere—that in itself is motivation for her to help us," Ramirez said.

"Did you notice when her hand went to that necklace? Looked like real silver to me, not stainless," Celebrity said. "So, Bobby was most likely paid, but maybe he didn't spend all the money yet."

They processed the scenario as Ramirez drove.

"Stop at the Foo. We're running low on coffee," Celebrity said.

CELEBRITY AND RAMIREZ sat in front of the Chief's desk and laid out the business with Janet Carrolmath. The Chief appeared agreeable over the proposed plan. They just had to sit tight until their pigeon showed up and played her part.

"Let's go talk to Betty. I promised to keep her in the loop of the investigation," Chief Price said.

They all headed out the door to two cars and went down the boulevard to Diaz Circle. The Chief rang the doorbell, and Jenkins answered the door, back on the job.

"Everything okay, Jenkins?" the Chief asked as he stepped into the foyer followed by his employees.

"Quiet on the home front," the butler said. He led the

police to Betty's office, where they found her Zooming with someone. She held up a finger to them, told whoever she was speaking to she'd call him back, then disconnected Zoom.

"To what do I owe the pleasure of your visit, Chief Price?" Betty asked.

They sat in front of the desk and laid out the upcoming scenario.

"If this Janet woman shows up tomorrow and plays her part, I will give her a reward of five thousand dollars. That will go a long way in Little Pancake—maybe even get her and those kids out of there," Betty said.

"We will definitely use that as an incentive prior to her speaking to this Robert Fayette," the Chief said.

"What did you think of her, Celebrity?" Betty asked.

"She's so downtrodden. I don't know the circumstances of her landing in Little Pancake, but I have a feeling she had a much better life," Celebrity said. "She's motivated. Five grand can change her life. Get her and her kids on a better path, if she cooperates."

"I trust your judgement," Betty said. "You'll escort her over here when she finishes up at the station?"

"Yes, ma'am," Celebrity said.

JIMMY, Brian, Guppy and Maddy sat in the gazebo chilling out, or at least putting in an effort to chill out. All the attempts on his life, and Guppy almost being killed, had Jimmy twitchy.

"Where's a time machine when you need it?" Jimmy asked. They watched as a couple of squirrels duked it out in the oak trees. They flew from branch to branch while making their little barking sounds.

Maddy raced around the ledge when the squirrels took to the ground and ran a streak to the other side of the property and launched into another tree. Guppy squawked while watching the rodents.

"If you went back and changed things, you would not be living in Twinkle, and you would not have discovered Maddy and her talents," Brian stated.

"I hadn't thought of that. Nope, I definitely would not change that part of this craziness," Jimmy said. "Look at her. She seems like a normal cat at times. I can't imagine how a cat could learn to communicate the way she does."

"We should do a study. Go to the animal shelter and adopt a couple of cats and sit them in front of the TV like Maddy," Brian said.

"Kittens, not adult cats. She's been watching children's programs since she was five or six weeks old. Something definitely changed in her brain," Jimmy said. "Who's going to take care of these kittens? I've already got two pets."

"Never mind. I can see the error of my ways," Brian said.

"COPS!" Guppy squawked out.

Jimmy and Brian noticed Celebrity walking across the lawn approaching the gazebo.

"Hi, guys!" she called out. She let herself into the gazebo and plunked down onto one of the built-in benches.

Maddy jumped onto her lap. "Hello, sweetheart." She scratched the kitten under her chin and behind the ears. Maddy's purring engine went into high gear.

Guppy, this could be our Mommy! Maddy exclaimed, which sounded like a few meows looped together.

"We've got a lead," Celebrity said. She explained the plan.

"With Aunt Betty's reward dangling in front of that woman, she'll go the extra distance to get every bit of information from her boyfriend, or husband, whatever the relation-ship," Jimmy said.

"I agree. Without the reward, who knows whether the amount the perp received—or even if any of it remains—would be enough to make that woman put any real effort into the plan," Celebrity said.

"I hope she shows up tomorrow morning," Brian said.

"She will. I have faith in her," Celebrity said.

Guppy walked around the ledge until he was beside Celebrity. He groomed her hair with his beak.

Celebrity laughed at the odd feeling. "He's not going to pull my hair out, is he?"

"You should feel honored. It's not every day an Amazon parrot will groom someone other than the person he lives with," Jimmy said.

Celebrity reached up a hand and patted Guppy's chest. "I love you too, Guppy."

"LOVE!" the bird boomed out.

THE FOLLOWING MORNING ARRIVED, but Janet didn't. They all watched the various clocks and their cell-phones as time ticked by. At nine-twenty, Celebrity's phone rang. She snatched it up. "Masters."

"Ms. Masters? It's Janet Carrolmath. My car broke down. I'm stranded at the side of the road on 44 and my phone's about to conk out."

"Stay with your car, Janet. I'll come get you in a regular car," Celebrity said. She disconnected the call and turned to her anxious audience. "Her car broke down over on 44. I'll go get her."

"This gives you the perfect opportunity to tell her about the reward," the Chief said. "But be cautious. This also could be a setup to get you alone."

Celebrity stood, removed her pistol from the holster, spun it and flipped it back into her holster like an Old West gunslinger. "I've got it covered. See you soon."

She got into her personal vehicle, a RAV4, and headed out. Fifteen minutes later, she spotted a rusted hunk on the side of the road. She pulled up behind the car, and a moment later, Janet slid into the passenger seat, teary.

"Thank you for coming to get me," the frazzled woman said as she buckled up.

Celebrity looked at her passenger, long and hard. She softened her face. "Janet, how did you end up in Little Pancake? I have the distinct feeling you have not always lived like this."

The woman burst into tears. "We used to live in a nice house. My husband worked as a driller, and he was killed in an accident at work. The company said it was because of his own negligence, so I didn't get any insurance money."

Celebrity grabbed tissues from a box in her console and placed some into Janet's hand.

Janet wiped her face and blew her nose. "Thanks. I was a stay-at-home mom and didn't have a career. I couldn't pay the mortgage, so I lost the house, and we were tossed to the curb."

"How did you end up with Robert Fayette?"

"He worked with my husband and took us in. We've been living with his father for the past five months. I can't imagine what this is doing to my kids," the woman wailed.

"Where's your phone? You can plug it into the charger," Celebrity said.

Janet rummaged in her purse, pulled the phone out and plugged it in. "Thank you for being so nice to me."

"Your guardian angel sure is looking out for you. Mrs. Diaz is prepared to pay you a reward of five thousand dollars for your help," Celebrity said. "She wants me to bring you over to her place when you are finished up at the station."

"Five thousand dollars?" Janet was numb thinking of what she could do with that money. "I don't think I'll be able to get us into an apartment because I don't have a job."

"We'll work on that after you help us this morning," Celebrity said. She shifted into reverse, backed the car up and made a U-turn.

They arrived at the police station and went inside.

CHAPTER SEVENTEEN

They decided to change tactics so that any information gained from Robert Fayette would be helpful in the overall criminal case of the mystery person. Instead of Janet wearing a wire, the interview would take place in the interrogation room with the recording system. Bobby would have a public defender, and Janet would have Celebrity, the Chief and Ramirez on her side of the table.

First, they introduced Bobby to Junior Stonerich, who worked for DDS, but had not made partner yet, so he was chosen as public defender. They spent a half an hour discussing Bobby's problem and the forthcoming visit with Janet.

At the designated time, Chief Price led Janet and his associates into the room. He motioned for Janet to take a seat across from Bobby. He walked over to the recording device and pressed some buttons. The interview would be audio and video recorded.

"Today is Thursday, June 18. I'm Police Chief Kenton Price. With me are Janet Carrolmath, Officer Celebrity Masters and Detective Benito Ramirez. On the other side of the table are Robert (Bobby) Fayette and Junior Stonerich, his court-appointed attorney."

The Chief took a seat at the far end of the table close to the equipment.

There were cameras mounted on the ceiling to show body and facial expressions of all parties.

Bobby, with a bandage on his chin from where Guppy bit him, appeared slightly shellshocked as the Chief started.

"Bobby, we're trying to get to the person responsible for these attacks on Jimmy Katz, the Katz-Diaz heir. With your help, no one else has to end up in a jail cell. Did your attorney inform you what your help would accomplish for you?" the Chief asked.

Bobby's eyes had been stationary on Janet but swung over to the Chief. "Yeah, he said I could get out of jail with a misdemeanor and probation for the B&E and a couple of months community service."

"Are you willing to help us with this case?" Detective Ramirez asked.

Again, Bobby looked at Janet.

"Bobby, someone's using you and those other guys," Janet said. "Whoever it is, they're hiring a bunch of amateurs instead of doing the work themselves. How much did they pay you?"

"A thousand bucks," he said.

"How did you get involved?" Janet asked.

"Found an ad in the paper," Bobby said.

"In the Twinkle newspaper?" the Chief asked, not quite keeping his shocked expression under control.

"Nah, that little community paper," Bobby said.

"Did you meet with the person who ran the ad?" Chief Price asked.

"Nah, I had to call a phone number," Bobby said.

"Was it a man's or woman's voice?" Chief Price asked.

"It was one of those robot voices," Bobby said.

"What did it say?" the Chief asked.

"Wanted me to go to the boarding house, toss things around and mess up the furniture to scare some guy so he'd move back to The Big City," Bobby said.

"How were you paid if you never met the person who hired you?" the Chief asked.

"He told me to go to the library and find this book, and the money would be inside the book," Bobby said.

"Did you spend all the money?" Janet asked. She gave slitted eyes to the Chief for stealing the show from her.

"I still got eight hundred," Bobby said.

"Where is it? I need to buy groceries, and refill your father's prescriptions," she said.

"I'd better not find that money missing when I get home, Janet," Bobby warned.

She glared at him across the table, pushed her chair back and walked out of the room, followed by Celebrity.

"Do you recall the name of the book and what section it was in?" the Chief asked.

"Yeah, it was a weird book in the reference section. *The Physiology of Ocean Bottom Feeders*," he said.

"Do you still have the ad from the paper?" the Chief asked.

"Probably."

"Where is it?"

"In my car."

Detective Ramirez left the room.

Twenty minutes later, Bobby was returned to his cell, and the meeting broke up. He would be released from jail in the morning.

"Get a search warrant for the car and the mobile home—we need to make sure we follow protocol," the Chief said.

Ramirez had the clunker that quit on Janet towed in so they could search through the trash and find the community paper ad.

"Okay, we have some useful information," the Chief said. He focused on Janet. "I appreciate your help, Janet. I truly hope your life turns around so you and your kids can get a new start."

"I was happy to help. People in Little Pancake aren't bad

people. They're just destitute like me and that drives them to do crazy things," she said.

"Let's go see Mrs. Diaz," Celebrity said. She led Janet out of the police station.

"How are we going to go about this with the library?" Ramirez asked.

"That was a clever setup. Voice scrambling software. Pickup in a public place," the Chief said. "We'll have to strategize."

"Do you think we could get those other two to talk?" Ramirez asked. "Especially Reuben Brown. He probably holds the tie between The Big City attorney and the Twinkle person."

CELEBRITY PRESSED THE DOORBELL AT THE mansion. Janet was awestruck as she heard the impressive gong reverberating throughout the house. Jenkins opened the door in his immaculate butler's livery.

"Good morning, Officer Masters. Mrs. Diaz is expecting you and your guest," the butler said. He led them to the office where Betty was typing on the computer. "Officer Masters and her guest are here to see you, Mrs. Diaz."

"Come in. Please have a seat. Jenkins, please bring us a tray of coffee articles," Betty said. Jenkins knew that was her way of telling him to add pastries, brownies, or cake to the tray.

Jenkins tipped his head and left the room, and Celebrity and Janet sat.

"I've never met a real butler before," Janet confessed. "He's so polite."

"Jenkins trained at the exclusive British Butler Institute in London," Betty explained.

"He's an American. A lot of men and women train in London for positions similar to Jenkins'," Betty said.

Celebrity jumped in before more chitchat continued. "Mrs. Diaz, this is Janet Carrolmath. We've just come from the police station where her friend is being held for his misdemeanor activity involving Jimmy's apartment. With Janet's help, her friend told the Chief how he was hired, and about other pertinent information."

Betty looked Janet over. "Well, Ms. Carrolmath, we have a lot to talk about. I am very grateful for your help. I just want to keep my great-nephew and myself safe. We're the last of the Katz's and he is my only direct heir."

They spent the next hour discussing Janet's dilemma and how Mrs. Diaz would help her. Janet left crying happy tears. Not only did she have a check for five grand in her purse, but Betty would find her work and a place to live within the next twenty-four hours, and she and her kids could stay in a hotel tonight for free.

Once Celebrity and Janet were out the door, Betty called the Chief and set up a meeting to discuss Janet's husband's death. She smelled a rat and felt certain that Grady Carrolmath was the fall guy. Since he was dead, he couldn't defend himself.

When the Chief sat across the desk from her, Betty laid out the cards of the situation. "I feel certain that Janet is due compensation for her husband's death. Do you think you can uncover what actually happened?"

The Chief nodded. "Most coverups are not sealed in concrete, even though they think they are. We'll get to the bottom of this."

The Chief left, then Betty got busy with Janet's current

problem. She called FeBe Morales over at the bank. "FeBe, we need to help a woman and her two children. By any chance, do you have a three-bedroom house in your possession that you'd like to fill?" She listened. "It's not a dump, is it?" She listened some more. "Oh, Hummingbird Heights is a nice middle-class neighborhood."

Next, she considered employment for someone who had been a homemaker, but decided she needed to have a conversation with Janet before she tried to help. Instead, she called Celebrity.

"Would you text me Janet's phone number?" Betty told Celebrity about the Chief investigating Grady's death.

JIMMY DROPPED IN AT HIS AUNT'S MANSION AND found her in the conservatory stretching. "Hi, Aunt Betty."

"Hello Jimmy. This has been a productive day." She told him about the police goings on with Janet and Bobby, that she had talked to the Chief about Janet's husband, and discovered that Janet had always wanted to be an interior designer. She arranged for Janet to take online classes on a new laptop that would be delivered as soon as she was moved into her new furnished living quarters in Hummingbird Heights.

"Wow, Aunt Betty, your philanthropy is amazing. That poor woman! I've seen Little Pancake. I can't imagine how difficult it must have been after her husband died."

"Jimmy, when I'm gone, I expect you to continue with my foundation work. We do not need yachts, limos or jets. We have within our power to change many people's lives," Betty said.

"I promise I will follow in your footsteps, Aunt Betty. I

don't need an expensive car or a lot of glitz—to me that puts a target on your back. I like living a low-keyed life," Jimmy said.

"Tomorrow I'll bring lunch to your place so I can spend some time getting to know your bird and kitten," Betty said.

"That would be great! We can have lunch, then go out to the gazebo," he said.

JUNIOR STONERICH SAT IN THE SAME interrogation room with Reuben Brown, Chief Price, Celebrity and Ramirez. Reuben presented a macho attitude until the Chief reminded him of his circumstances. Then the pretense dropped, replaced with a sullen face.

"Reuben, as your attorney most likely discussed with you earlier, we have linked you to an armed robbery at a gas station in The Big City. Security cameras show you holding up Jimmy Katz' at pump number eight at gunpoint, then stealing his vehicle," the Chief stated. "Then, it appears that whoever hired you had you come to Twinkle, my jurisdiction, where you broke into Mr. Katz' apartment to inflict harm."

Reuben shifted in his chair but kept quiet.

"We would appreciate it if you would disclose your employer. If you were paid for these jobs, you have no way of accessing your money. You aren't going to be released from my jail anytime soon, and if your money is in your place back in The Big City instead of in the bank, you're more than likely going to lose it unless someone pays your rent while you're incarcerated."

The lightbulb appeared to come on in Mr. Brown's head.

"Who contacted you about the gas station robbery?" the Chief asked.

Junior whispered into Reuben's ear.

"I saw this ad in the neighborhood paper," Reuben said. "I called the phone number and a weird voice answered—it echoed loudly. I couldn't tell if it was a man or woman."

"What instructions were you given, and did you meet someone to get paid?" The Chief, Celebrity and Ramirez knew the answers, but waited patiently. If even one thing differed, it might be a link to a new lead.

"The voice said to go to the downtown library and find this weird book. That's where further instructions and the money would be," Reuben said.

"What was the title of the book, do you remember?" the Chief asked.

"Something about Ocean Bottom Feeders. It was in the reference section way up high and I had to get one of those rolling stepping stools to get it down," Reuben said.

"What did the instructions tell you?" the Chief asked.

"I had to follow this car until a good opportunity came up, then rob the guy to scare him off, and to take his car, then torch it," Reuben said.

"Why did you throw the briefcase out of the car?" the Chief asked.

"The instructions didn't say anything about a briefcase, so I figured I'd be merciful," Reuben said with a snarky attitude, as if to say that he did someone a big favor.

"How were you contacted about this Twinkle job?" the Chief asked.

"I got a text that told me to go back to the library," Reuben said. "There were instructions and more money in the same book."

"What did the instructions say this time?" the Chief asked.

"I had to drive to Twinkle, to this boarding house, get the ladder out of the tool shed and go in through the window. I had to look Twinkle up on the map... never heard of it," Reuben said. "It was so dark I could hardly see my hand in front of my face!"

"You never communicated or met anyone in person? Only with the voice on the phone, or in text messages?" the Chief asked.

"That's the way it happened," Reuben said.

"Okay, thank you for the information. We'll deliberate. It will be noted in your file that you cooperated," the Chief said.

He, Celebrity, and Ramirez stood.

"I'd like a moment with my client," Junior said. "In private, with the recording devices turned off."

The Chief stopped the recording, and then he and his team left the interrogation room. An officer stood outside the door, waiting to return Mr. Brown to his cell.

"Okay, we have the same type of setup. Ramirez, you, and Celebrity get to our library and find that book. See if you can get prints. I'll call Detective Breeland and see if he can access that book in The Big City downtown library. Hopefully, no one has touched it since Mr. Brown," the Chief said. He had a moment. "Oh, check Brown's cellphone. It should be in with his personal effects. Those texts were probably from a throw-away phone, but let's make sure."

Ramirez and Celebrity took off, and the Chief shut himself into his office. He looked up Detective Breeland's phone number and placed the call.

"Breeland," the detective said when he answered his cellphone.

"Detective Breeland? Kenton Price from Twinkle here. I wanted to thank you for the electronic files. We've been busy putting together a chain of events that paints a much larger picture that includes embezzlement of millions of dollars, attempted murder, possibly murder, and a few other things. The attorney on your end is culpable, but we're still searching for the master planner. We need your help," the Chief said.

He laid out the results of the interrogation of Reuben Brown. They discussed the community paper and the possibility that more than one person could have called the number. They also discussed Breeland getting a search warrant for Reuben's apartment to find the community paper and any other evidence. Then they discussed the library and the particular book.

"I'll get the search warrant for the apartment, but I won't need one for the library book. That's public property," Breeland said. "I hope we can find your link."

CHAPTER EIGHTEEN

R amirez and Celebrity entered the Twinkle Public Library. They studied the layout of the library and found the reference section. They carefully went up and down rows in search of the section including marine life. At long last, they were in the correct section.

Celebrity took one side of the bookshelves, Ramirez took the other side. Back-to-back, they tediously searched shelves from floor to over their heads. Those higher shelves were attained with a rolling step stool.

"Getting a crick in my neck," Ramirez said.

They both met at the end shelves. Celebrity turned around and was startled to see that the chief librarian's glassed-in office was at the top of the stairs in direct sight of where they stood.

"Ramirez, turn around and tell me what you see," Celebrity said.

Ramirez turned around in time to see Divinia Reynolds walk into her office with someone. He turned back around. "Hhmmm. That's a coincidence."

They continued searching for the book. Ramirez found it on the top shelf in the middle. He pulled gloves out of his pocket and carefully pried the book off the shelf, holding the top edges so as not to smudge any fingerprints.

Celebrity held open an evidence bag and Ramirez carefully slid the book into the bag. They turned to exit the section and spotted Divinia at the top of the stairs with her eyes on them.

"Quick, get the Chief on the horn. If she's our mastermind, we have to get a search warrant for her house and property, and her office here before she destroys evidence," Ramirez said.

Celebrity was one step ahead of him. She speed-texted the Chief and laid out their suspicions. He texted her back that he would personally go see Judge Moore and get the warrants. They were to proceed with questioning Divinia and keeping her otherwise occupied.

Ramirez and Celebrity headed to the stairs. Divinia turned and hurried toward an exit. Ramirez sped up and caught her at a door.

"I'm sorry, but I have a meeting and need to rush," the librarian said.

"Ma'am, you're going to have to miss that meeting. We are going to have to take you to the police station for questioning," Ramirez said.

Celebrity joined them. She held up her cell phone. "I have a warrant to search your office and your home. Is anyone at your home right now?"

"Search warrants?" The panic was evident in the librarian's voice and demeanor. Her cool exterior shattered as she realized her game was up.

Celebrity entered the librarian's office.

Ramirez gripped Divinia's arm. "You have a choice, Divinia. Either you let me escort you out to the car, or you go out handcuffed. Which will it be?"

He nudged her away from the fire exit door and brought her to the main staircase. They walked down the stairs and out the front door, where he settled her into the back seat of the car. Ramirez called the Chief once the librarian was secured. "Celebrity is searching the office. I have Divinia in the car. Want me to bring her in?"

"Yes. I'm on my way to the library. Celebrity and I can finish up there, then head out to Divinia's house," the Chief said.

Just as they disconnected their call, the Chief's car pulled up and parked beside Ramirez's police car. They nodded to each other. The Chief got out of his car and hurried into the library.

CELEBRITY SAT AT THE DESK FLIPPING THROUGH papers in file folders as the Chief entered the office.

"Anything?" he asked.

"Not yet, but there's a ton of paperwork," she said.

The Chief pulled a chair around to the other side of the desk and started on those drawers. Celebrity scooted her chair over to give him some room.

The first drawer contained office supplies. The second drawer had snacks. The bottom file drawer had file folders of employees. He pulled out several blue Pendaflex folders stuffed with Manila file folders, and set them on the corner of the desk in front of him. Each Manila folder had an employee's name at the top typed on a label.

Chief Price started going through each folder and scrutinized the contents. There were full-time employees, volunteers, part-time employees, maintenance staff and companies that performed services, such as air conditioning and heating, and an elevator company.

On the other side of the desk, Celebrity was startled when she read Josie Rigton's name on a folder. She flipped past it and discovered Reuben Brown's name, then Robert Fayette, and Dickie Mutulant. The last folder was titled Wilkinson. The officer was about to put all the irrelevant folders back in the drawer when she spotted what looked like a newspaper classified page with a big red circle around an ad and some handwriting.

Celebrity reached in and pulled out the newspaper. There

were people's names and phone numbers written in blue ink by the circled ad.

"We've got her!" Celebrity said.

"Put those in an evidence bag," the Chief said. "We need to go through the rest of these files to see what they contain. These might not be employees."

Celebrity grabbed all the folders and slid them into evidence bags along with the classified page.

JIMMY ACCOMPANIED Ramirez and Sgt. Garcia to Divinia Reynolds' house on Pansy Avenue. Ramirez rang the doorbell. "Police! I have a warrant to search the premises," he called out.

No one answered. Jimmy motioned that he would check the outside of the house.

Ramirez pulled tools out of his pocket and picked the lock. He and Sgt. Garcia entered the house while pulling on gloves. It was quiet. They went through the house searching for anyone who might be hidden inside. Sgt. Garcia took the upstairs and Ramirez downstairs. Once they determined no one was hiding, they began to search in earnest.

Jimmy tapped on the door.

Ramirez opened the door.

"I looked through the garage window and there's a Toyota 4Runner in there. Could be Josie Rigton's vehicle. Also, there's some new landscaping in the backyard," Jimmy said.

They both jumped to the same conclusion—Josie could very well be planted in the backyard.

"Sarge!" Ramirez called out. "We've got a situation."

Sgt. Garcia ran down the stairs. "What's up?" He listened

as Ramirez called the Chief and told him what Jimmy had discovered.

THE CHIEF LEFT CELEBRITY IN CHARGE OF THE EVIDENCE gleaned from the library desk files, and rushed down the stairs and out the front door of the library. He turned on the flashing lights and siren and sped out of the parking lot. He arrived at Divinia's house in less than five minutes.

They observed the old black Toyota 4Runner from the garage window. Sgt. Garcia went inside and pushed the garage door opener, and the door climbed the tracks. Ramirez opened the passenger door, then the glove box, searching for the vehicle registration. He found documentation showing the vehicle's owner.

"It's Josie Rigton's," Ramirez said.

They all walked to the backyard where new landscaping had just been planted.

"Could be," the Chief said. "Have you finished going through the house yet?"

"No, we just started when Jimmy found the truck," Ramirez said.

"Let me get CSI out here. We need all the help we can get," the Chief said. He filled them in as to what he discovered in the library desk, then he texted CSI Lloyd.

The Chief and Jimmy donned gloves, and they all returned to the house.

"We need to find any evidence that Divinia may have hidden away, along with any evidence that Josie didn't leave here. Just because her truck is here doesn't mean much. She could have asked Divinia if she could park it in the garage while she was out of town," the Chief said.

"Okay," Ramirez said. "How do you want to split this up? Master bedroom is downstairs. There's two bedrooms upstairs."

"Is there a home office?" Jimmy asked.

"I didn't see one upstairs," Sgt. Garcia said.

"There's just the small desk in the living room," Ramirez said.

"Garcia, you and Jimmy take the upstairs. Examine and bag every scrap of paper you come across," the Chief said. "Ramirez, you take her bedroom. I'll take the living room. We can tackle the kitchen last."

Just as they were getting ready to split up, the doorbell rang. The Chief went to the door and looked through the viewer and saw CSI Lloyd. He opened the door.

"Hey, Chief. What do we have?" Lloyd asked.

They discussed the truck in the garage, the new landscaping, and their approach to searching the house.

"Any evidence of blood anywhere?" Lloyd asked.

"Not that I'm aware of, but we just got here. Ramirez and Garcia did a cursory look to check for occupation and didn't find anyone. We haven't checked the garage, other than getting into the glovebox to see who the vehicle was registered to," the Chief said.

"Let me go shine my light in the garage and see if I find any blood. I'll check around the exterior of the house, too," Lloyd said.

The Chief tackled the desk first. It was just a small desk with a typical long middle drawer in front, and two small drawers on each side. It didn't contain file drawers. He sat in the chair and pulled out the long middle drawer. There were pencils and scraps of paper. He checked the pieces of paper and bagged them. He lifted up the table lamp. There wasn't anything under it. He turned it over to see if anything was stuffed underneath. There wasn't. The Chief opened the top right drawer.

There was a knock on the front door. The Chief stopped what he was doing and opened the door.

"Sorry. Door was locked. I found a garbage bag in the trash can inside the garage with bloody clothes in it," Lloyd said.

"We've got blood in the garage," the Chief called out.

Ramirez rushed out of the bedroom, and Garcia and Jimmy thundered down the stairs.

"Ramirez, get Peterson and Dupont over here," the Chief said. He turned to CSI Lloyd. "Get your whole team over here. We'll need shovels. Looks like a fresh grave with landscaping on top, so probably not very deep."

Danny Stonerich's car pulled up. People were rubber-necking in vehicles, and neighbors walked down the sidewalk and gathered.

"What's happening? Did you arrest Divinia Reynolds? Is she the mastermind for all the incidents with Jimmy?"

"Jimmy, help Garcia string up the yellow crime scene tape. Need to keep the neighbors out of the way," the Chief barked out. "Danny, we don't have time to talk to you right now."

"Can I at least take pictures if I promise to stay out of the way?" Danny asked. This was the biggest crime story to hit their paper, and he wanted to get as much information as possible. He called his father.

The Chief grunted. Danny took that to mean he could take pictures.

Celebrity arrived, followed by Peterson, Dupont, and Lloyd's team. Cases of equipment were grabbed by the CSI team. Lloyd directed them to the garage and the backyard.

Ramirez and Garcia grabbed the shovels from the back of the CSI vehicle and brought them to the backyard.

Danny followed at a respectable distance so he wouldn't get kicked out of the yard. His eyes widened as he put two and two together. Shovels, new landscaping, the truck in the garage. He got his father on the phone.

"Dad! I think Josie Rigton was murdered and buried in Divinia's backyard! I'll report back soon. I'm taking pictures while I still have access. Send Ag or someone—I can't be in two places at once!"

Jimmy stood with the Chief as the CSI team took pictures of the newly turned earth and the azalea bushes. They discussed the route taken from the garage to the current location.

Lloyd and his team shone special lights on the scene, searching for even a drop of blood. They worked in a wide swath from the back door of the garage to the landscaping. During their search, they uncovered a series of blood droplets on the grass, which they circled with spray paint.

When the trail ended at the landscaping, there was no doubt as to what happened and who was buried under the azaleas. They carefully removed the three newly planted four-gallon azalea bushes and set them aside. Lloyd assigned two of his team to the shovels. It was easy digging, as the grave was so new and the dirt still relatively loose.

Three feet down, they hit something solid. Lloyd got into the shallow hole and straddled whatever was down there. He used his hands to scoop dirt and fling it out of the grave. Team members joined him. They discovered the body wrapped in a bright green shower curtain. Everyone climbed out of the grave.

One of the CSI members took pictures from several angles before the body was removed.

The Chief and Jimmy approached the gravesite. "Damn shame," the Chief said.

"This is going to crush Aunt Betty," Jimmy said. "Why'd Divinia have to kill Josie? Why couldn't she have given her a bus ticket to New Jersey or somewhere?"

"Insane people can't be counted on to do rational things," the Chief said.

They left the gravesite CSI team to their work and walked back to the house, with Danny following at a respectable distance. Camera flashes lit up the dark garage.

Celebrity helped erect an enclosure for the CSI team. They needed a sheltered space so they could go through the garbage can without the public witnessing the procedure or the gruesome contents. When the structure was anchored, they spread plastic on the ground, then carried the garbage container to the center of the secluded area. On top of the bloody black garbage bag were several bloody cloths and paper towels.

"She probably wiped her hands and just tossed those on top of the bag," Jimmy said. "You'd think she'd hide those in at least a grocery bag. It's a lot of blood to explain away, say, for a cut on the finger."

"Maybe she planned to do that later," Celebrity said.

"I want to know what sort of weapon was used. Did Divinia shoot her? Stab her? How did she kill her?" Jimmy asked.

"We'll know soon enough," the Chief said grimly. "Let's get back to the house. There's still a lot to do."

Everyone replaced their gloves. They spread out upstairs and on the first floor, combing every inch of the place. Any scrap of paper was placed in evidence bags from any other physical evidence.

Lloyd entered the house and approached the Chief. Jimmy

saw him and hurried over. "Victim was stabbed in the back six times. Not sure what was used, but I'm confident we'll find the weapon. I'll examine the steering wheel of the Toyota to see if the killer is the one who drove the 4Runner into the garage."

"I'm going to guess that Josie probably came over here for money so she could leave town, and Divinia killed her as she was trying to get away," Jimmy said as he thought out loud.

"Sounds reasonable. I'm certain we'll get the complete story once I interrogate Divinia," the Chief said.

Several hours passed as the entire scene was processed. Mrs. Potts had arrived at the midpoint with Brian. They carried large platters of sandwiches and brownies, and a big coffee machine one would typically use at a large event. Brian set up a long folded table not too far away from an outlet at the front door. He plugged in the coffee machine, then returned to the car for the paper cups and stir sticks.

"We really appreciate you going to all this trouble, Mrs. Potts," Chief Price said.

"Chief Price, I'm devastated, as the town will be when they find out our head librarian had plotted to get her hands on the Katz-Diaz fortune! Do you know what sent Divinia on this rampage?" Mrs. Potts asked.

The Chief hung his head. "It's definitely put a blight on our town, but we can overcome it. People love Betty and what she's done for the town and county."

Jimmy wandered over. "I can't get my head around this whole thing. I hope Aunt Betty hasn't heard about Josie. While she's upset and probably a little angry that Josie was involved in this plot, she would never, ever wish her dead!"

"We should go talk to her before the radio station announces something," the Chief said.

Jimmy and the Chief left in separate cars and drove over to Diaz Circle.

CHAPTER NINETEEN

Jenkins led the Chief and Jimmy back to Betty's office. She took note of the tight expressions on their faces.

"Where'd you find Josie? West Texas? Colorado?" Betty asked.

"At Divinia's house," the Chief said.

"Divinia was harboring a fugitive?" Betty squawked out. "Why would she do that?"

"Aunt Betty, I'm sorry to have to tell you this, but Divinia killed Josie," Jimmy said as gently as he could.

Betty pushed back from the desk. "No!" She turned to the Chief. "How?"

"I haven't interrogated her yet, but the house and property tell the story. Jimmy discovered Josie's vehicle in the garage, and new landscaping in the backyard. CSI Lloyd discovered bloody clothes in a garbage can in the garage. At this point, I don't know if Divinia killed her in the house or garage, then dragged her out to the backyard," the Chief said.

"They're still going through the house, Aunt Betty," Jimmy said. "We didn't want you to hear about it on the radio."

"Was she working with The Big City attorney?" Betty asked.

"We're not there yet, but if anything, I'd bet that Divinia is the one who enticed him into the scheme," the Chief said. "I have a detective friend in The Big City who is working on that."

"At least there won't be any more problems," Jimmy said.

"I hate to be the bearer of bad news, but until we know for certain that no other people answered her ad and were hired, we will have to be very cautious. My team has its work cut out for them, matching people to her list," the Chief said.

Betty buried her face in her hands. "I hate to break this news to my staff. They are going to be shocked at this turn of events. It was bad enough thinking that someone who worked for me for a decade would try to kill me."

The Chief stood. "I'm sorry, Betty. I'd better get back to the station."

"I appreciate you stopping by. I would have most likely fainted if I'd heard that on the news," Betty said.

Jimmy lingered. "Are you going to be okay?"

"I'm heartbroken over this whole situation, but there was no way I could have seen this coming. Never in my wildest thoughts could I have envisioned these events," Betty said. She stood. "You'd better go attend to your animals. I owe you a lunch and a gazebo visit."

"Mrs. Potts was taking care of them, so they'll be okay for a little longer. I'm going back to Divinia's house." Jimmy hugged her, then took off.

IT WAS DARK WHEN JIMMY CLIMBED THE PORCH STAIRS and unlocked the boarding house door. He followed Guppy's voice to the kitchen. Maddy rushed up to him and stood on her hind legs, begging to be picked up. She had one paw on one side of his neck and the other on the other side in her version of a hug.

Oh, Daddy! You're so stressed! Maddy meowed several times.

Mrs. Potts and Brian were drinking iced tea at the table.

Jimmy flopped into a chair, and Maddy settled onto his lap.

"Well, buddy, this was some adventure," Brian said. "I

think I'm totally over my bad breakup. Now I just need to figure out what I'm going to do with myself."

"There's an opening at the TIN," Jimmy said. "I could put in a good word with Sylvan and Bill."

Brian let that swirl around in his head. "I really like a smaller town. The Big City just pushed over to seven million people. You know how crowded those roads were? I don't miss it one bit."

"Cooking for three is much easier than cooking for two," Mrs. Potts said with a huge smile.

CHIEF PRICE PLACED a call to The Big City. "Detective Breeland?" He brought him up to date on the most recent happenings in Twinkle. "We found a file on Wilkinson that outlines his role. I'm going to talk to the DA about issuing a warrant for his arrest, so you may hear from us soon."

Norbert Jones, the Twinkle district attorney, wasted no time getting in touch with The Big City boys. He mentioned Detective Breeland acted as the intermediary between their jurisdictions when he talked to The Big City DA. A warrant was issued for the arrest of Joseph Wilkinson, and he was taken into custody.

Detective Breeland also had search warrants for Wilkinson's office and home. A separate police unit was headed to the house as the attorney was hauled off in a police car.

The detective and Officer Davis secured the office and thoroughly searched files, drawers, and cabinets. Breeland discovered a lockbox bolted in a corner of a cabinet. He returned to the desk and searched in the drawers and other obvious places for a key. Breeland found a small, silver-colored key hidden among paperclips. He fished it out, returned to the cabinet, and slipped it into the lockbox. It unlocked the box. He flipped the lid open and found stacks of banded bills with the face of Ben Franklin smirking up at him.

He pulled the banded stacks out of the box. There was a sheet of paper at the bottom of the box with dates and some sort of code. Now, all he needed was the paper trail to link the illegal money to the cash in the box and to decode the numbers.

"Davis," Breeland called out. "Do you have a flashlight and some tools?"

"In the car. Be right back," Davis called back.

Breeland heard the outer door open and close. Davis returned with a high-powered flashlight and a tool kit.

"Found a stash of cash in a lockbox that's attached to the cabinet. Can you work on that while I search for the decoding doc?" Breeland asked.

"Sure thing," Davis said. He got on his hands and knees and pulled a smaller flashlight out of the toolkit, then wedged himself into the cabinet. It was tight for the wide-shouldered officer. He backed his shoulders out, then commenced to remove the screws that secured the cabinet door, set the door aside, then began to assess how the box was attached to the bottom of the cabinet. Before long, Davis had the lockbox removed and inside an evidence bag.

Breeland crab-walked around the floor, opening cabinets and shining the flashlight in every corner. He happened to flash the light up and discovered a Manila envelope taped to the top of the underside of the cabinet in the shadowed corner.

"Bingo," the detective said. He carefully pried the tape and envelope loose, then backed up and stood. "Let's see what secrets you hold." He walked over to the attorney's desk and used the letter opener to slit the envelope open.

The damning evidence was all there. Communications from Divinia. The code for the other sheet of paper in the lockbox. His hangman's noose. Breeland pulled his phone out and placed a call to Twinkle.

"Chief Price? Breeland here. Wilkinson is in custody. I've just discovered a lockbox with a hell of a lot of money in it along with a list of codes, but that's not all. I just discovered a hidden envelope with all of his communications with Divinia Reynolds and the decoding list."

CHIEF PRICE ENDED THE CALL WITH BREELAND ON A happy note. He immediately called Jimmy. "You'll be happy to know your old family attorney, Joseph Wilkinson, is in custody and evidence is being collected. It will hang him and Divinia."

"I can't wait until I can look him in the eye while I tell him he's going to rot in prison," Jimmy said.

The next day the TIN headline stated:

CONSPIRACY UNCOVERED!
TWINKLE HEAD LIBRARIAN CHARGED IN KATZ-DIAZ FORTUNE CAPER

After Jimmy, Brian and Mrs. Potts read the article by Danny and Sylvan Stonerich, Jimmy headed over to the mansion. Jenkins answered the door and led the heir to the conservatory.

Betty was standing on her head on a strange carved-out pillow.

Jenkins leaned in and whispered in Jimmy's ear. "She calls that her crown pillow." He winked, then left the room.

Betty righted herself, bringing her legs down to her shoulders, then down to her knees. She stood. "There's nothing like having the blood rush to your head and out again. You should try it sometime."

"I'll wait until I'm your age," he joked. "Did you see the paper this morning?"

"Yes, that was a very good article. I'll call Sylvan and commend him and Danny. I imagine the community is reeling over this conspiracy," Betty said. "When I had to break the news about Josie to my staff, they wandered around here like zombies. It was just too shocking."

"It goes to show you that it doesn't matter the size of the town; there are devious people everywhere," Jimmy said.

"Well, now that this situation is under control, and all parties are in jail, what are your plans? Will you return to the paper and continue to write articles?" Betty asked.

"I've been thinking about that. I'm going to continue my studies with Moses and Toombs, write at least one column for the TIN, and spend some time with DDS so I can learn about the foundations and how the estate is handled," Jimmy said. "Mr. Wilkinson was our family attorney forever. I still can't get over how he bilked me out of all that money."

"I understand," Betty said. "I encourage you to learn as much about the estate as you can. DDS will not let you down."

"What are you going to do today, Aunt Betty?"

"Jenkins is taking me over to the police department where I will face Divinia and ask her why she went down this road," she said.

"Can I come with you? I'd like to understand why she killed my parents," he said.

Betty patted his back. "Yes, why don't we go together. The whole situation is about family after all."

Jenkins drove them to the police department, and Betty entered through the door like a queen. Everyone greeted her with reverence in their tone and expressions.

"Sgt. Gonzales, is Chief Price available?" Betty asked at the front desk.

"Yes, ma'am. You can go back—Jimmy knows the way," Sgt. Gonzales said.

Betty didn't bother knocking on the door, which was open. She gracefully barreled into the office and stood in front of the desk. "Kenton, I want to see Divinia."

He looked her square in the eye. "Betty, do you think that's a good idea?"

"Of course, it is; otherwise, I wouldn't be standing in front of your desk," she said. "I need to hear her explanation about this whole setup so I can put it to rest."

"I don't know if she will agree to speak with you without her lawyer," the Chief said.

"Who did she hire?" Betty asked.

"Junior Stonerich—he's the public defender," the Chief said.

"Can you call and get him over here? It's not like he's going to be so tied up with clients in Twinkle," Betty said snidely.

"Okay, hold on a minute." The Chief picked up the office phone receiver and called DDS. "It's Chief Price. Is Junior available?" He waited while the call was being transferred. "Junior? Betty's in my office and she wants to talk to Divinia. I thought I'd better call you in case something is said that may further incriminate Divinia." He listened. "Okay. See you in a minute."

"See, that wasn't that difficult," Betty said.

The Chief placed an interoffice call. "Celebrity? Mrs. Diaz is going to speak with Divinia. Junior is on his way over. Could you bring the prisoner to the interrogation room?" He hung up the phone. "Give Celebrity a few minutes. Why don't you sit down while we wait for Junior?"

Jimmy and Betty sat in the chairs in front of the Chief's

desk. It was an odd silence—no one had anything more to say to each other.

Junior Stonerich entered the police station and walked back to the Chief's office. "Let me have a minute to speak with my client."

Several minutes later, Celebrity entered the Chief's office doorframe. "All set."

The Chief, Jimmy and Betty stood. "I'll accompany you." The Chief led Betty to the secure room and opened the door. The librarian was in handcuffs secured by a chain around her waist and down to the floor. Her feet were also secured. Junior Stonerich sat beside her.

Betty stared at the disheveled woman in an orange jump-suit cuffed to the chair. She entered the room further and sat in one of the chairs across from the librarian. Jimmy sat across from Junior. The Chief stood by the recording equipment.

"I'm recording this session. Agreed?" He looked at Junior, who nodded.

Divinia wore a hard expression on her face. She stared at Betty with complete loathing.

"Why?" Betty asked.

"I've worked at the library for my entire career, Betty. How could you pass us over? You didn't even include the Twinkle library in the estate to receive a bequest!"

"Is that what this was all about? I don't know how you got your hands on my will—I can only guess that Josie played a part in that, but obviously Josie never got her hands on the amendment document," Betty said.

"Amendment?" Divinia asked. It was obvious she had no knowledge of any amendment.

"Yes, Divinia. You see, I admired how you worked so hard to abolish illiteracy in our community, that I planned a whole new library building that would allow you to expand all the programs you so diligently plan each year," Betty said.

The librarian tried to lurch out of the chair. She screamed as if she were in agony as she realized what she had done.

Betty stood. Jimmy stood. They left the room and waited in the hallway for the Chief. When he exited the interrogation room, he took Betty's hand and wove it through his arm and guided her back to his office with Jimmy following in a daze.

"All this death and destruction over misinformation. So many lives altered," Betty said.

"It's over. You've got your explanation, Betty, and now we wait for the trial," the Chief said.

"So, I guess she had my parents killed because she thought my father was a threat standing between her and the estate?" Jimmy asked.

"Yes. Your father and you were my two heirs. I can't connect how she thought she was going to become the Katz-Diaz heir, even if she eliminated you and me," Betty said.

"I'll bet she thought Mr. Wilkinson could produce a new will," Jimmy said.

"Let's get out of here, Jimmy. I want to go home, and I imagine you want to go have a beer with Brian," Betty said.

"Or two," Jimmy said.

JIMMY SAT at the table with Brian and Mrs. Potts. Guppy was on the fourth chair back, and Maddy was curled in his lap. Two empty beer bottles stood in front of him.

"I'm glad that's over and done with and everyone who should be is in jail," Jimmy said.

"You really livened up the town, Jimmy," Mrs. Potts said.

"But I'm sure everyone will be happy to settle into a calmer life. We're just not used to this much crime!"

"Wait until the trial," Brian said.

"You going to move in permanently?" Jimmy asked his friend.

"Talked to Sylvan and Bill. They said Gigi wasn't coming back, so I'll be sitting in her chair come Monday."

"I'm thinking about asking Celebrity out," Jimmy said.

"Don't think—do!" Mrs. Potts said.

Maddy reached up and patted Jimmy's bottom lip.

The end... or is it?

BILL HILL'S PILLS

Here's what's happening in Twinkle, Texas.

Jimmy Katz wakes walloped with a cold, allergies, or the flu. Maddy, his cat, and Guppy, his Amazon parrot, fret, but still demand breakfast. Mrs. Potts sends Jimmy over to the Wellness Center where Bill Hill sends the Katz-Diaz heir home with his special formula, Wellness in a Bottle.

Brian, Jimmy's best friend, and Danny, his coworker at the Twinkle Independent News (TIN), come to visit, followed by Aunt Betty, the matriarch of Twinkle and Starlight County. Celebrity stops by, sees how awful Jimmy feels, and tells him she'll be back later.

The town drunk attacks Celebrity, and she ends up in a coma. When she resurfaces, a different reality has everyone concerned, especially Jimmy.

After only three doses of Bill Hill's formula, Jimmy fully recovers. He stops by the Wellness Center to purchase two more bottles. When he arrives home, Maddy and Guppy attack the bag. Then Brian and Danny show up and tell him that someone was poisoned by that formula.

The deranged poisoner has targeted more than Bill Hill's store. The Dime Water Foo(d) grocery store with the burned-out "d" in the sign, affectionately called the Foo, is shut down. It's the only grocery store within a 150-mile radius. Betty calls upon her army of volunteers, and they transform the Starlight Ballroom into a grocery store.

More businesses are shut down as tampered products send people to the hospital. Chief Kenton Price, Ramirez, and

Celebrity have their hands full trying to hunt down the elusive poisoner, along with help from the Feds. Through the investigation, they discover that forty years ago a terrible crime was committed and concealed. Jimmy and Ramirez uncover the details and seek justice for the family.

While eating at the Biggem Diner with Danny, Brian, Ramirez, and Celebrity, Jimmy notices the poisoner in action. Ramirez and Celebrity take action. The culprit has been arrested.

Here's a link to Bill Hill's Pills: https://www.degreenfield .com

Scroll down the page until you see the Twinkle, Texas Katz' Cat series.

ABOUT THE AUTHOR

 Dawn Greenfield Ireland is an award-winning author of 22 novels, including 5 series (cozy mystery, sci fi/fantasy, billionaire shapeshifters, and dystopian), and a stand-alone sci-fi romantic adventure.

Most of her 7 nonfiction books have won awards, and she has adapted a few of her screenplays into book format. She also created over 50 themed notebooks.

Two of her screenplays were optioned, and she worked on a screenwriter-for-hire project. Dawn has a certificate from the Professional Program in Screenwriting from UCLA (2002), and ScreenwritingU.

Dawn writes full-time. She lives among dreams and fantasies with two cats and moving boxes. Her head is filled with stories. She doesn't suffer from writer's block.

Her business, Artistic Origins, has been around since 1995. Besides writing, she coaches writers, edits, formats, and publishes clients' books.

Her former day job as an award-winning technical writer played a major role in her fiction writing. She is detail-oriented, the organizational queen of the known universe, and never misses a deadline.

Let me know if you find any bloopers I've missed.

Need an editor? Book formatter? Your book adapted into a screenplay? I'm your gal. Check out all my awards on my website, then click the Artistic Origins tab for all my services.

Please take the time to leave a review! Reviews help authors so much.

Sign up for the newsletter and get the inside scoop ahead of everyone else.

http://degreenfield.com

instagram.com/dawngreenfieldIreland

facebook.com/dawn.ireland.18

linkedin.com/in/degreenfield

goodreads.com/dawnireland

x.com/dawnireland

www.ingramcontent.com/pod-product-compliance
Lightning Source LLC
Chambersburg PA
CBHW020905180626
46816CB00007BA/2249